Deadly Hunger and Other Tales

Deadly Hunger and Other Tales

Joe L. Hensley

Five Star
Unity, Maine

Five Star First Edition Mystery Series.
Published in 2001 in conjunction with Tekno Books and Ed Gorman.

Copyright continued on page 220.

Set in 11 pt. Plantin.

Printed in the United States on permanent paper.

Library of Congress Cataloging-in-Publication Data

Hensley, Joe L., 1926–
    Deadly hunger and other tales / by Joe L. Hensley.
        p.   cm. — (Five Star first edition mystery series)
    ISBN 0-7862-3141-6 (hc : alk. paper)
    I. Detective and mystery stories, American. I. Title.
II. Series.
PS3558.E55 D43 2001
    813′.54—dc21   2001016000

Table of Contents

A Few Words. 7

Paint Doctor 10

Deadly Hunger 24

Widow. 37

A Lot of Sense 46

Argent Blood 60

Whistler 66

Watcher 80

Killer Scent 91

The Home 104

On the Rocks 121

The Calculator 127

Savant 141

Decision 156

Truly Yours, John R. Jacks 167

Trial 175

Shut the Final Door 185

The Retiree 194

Fifty Chinese 207

A Few Words

This is my twenty-first book, being my third short story collection, plus seventeen suspense novels, and one science fiction novel.

Let me remember:

A long time ago the car in front of mine skidded and hit an eighteen wheeler and both burst into flames. I avoided the wreck and pulled to the side of the road. A small boy about three years old sat dazed and tattered on the berm after being thrown from the car. Miraculously he had no severe injury. We both listened to his parents scream as they burned to death in white hot, gasoline heat. I put my Navy peacoat around the boy against the bitter cold and mercifully soon there were ambulances. He was a sole survivor and I write about him over and over. You may find him in this book.

At Truk in the central Caroline Islands at the tag end of WWII, I did independent duty as a hospital corpsman temporarily assigned to the Third Marine Division. Each day, after regular sick call, marine runners delivered me Japanese prisoners and I either painted them with merthiolate or gave them an A.P.C., by direction of authority.

There were headless U.S. fliers bodies found on Truk. Someone Japanese had cut the heads off.

I wrote about that in "Paint Doctor" and now I've no more desire to revisit the time. After all it's an old war and most of those who were in it are dead or dying and include me.

For fourteen years I sat on the bench and listened to the lies and truths of those accused of crime and those seeking damages. I wrote about the people I judged again and again. I used truths I learned along the way and turned them into fictions.

For those same fourteen years I did ninety percent of all hearings at the area mental hospitals. If the patients were dangerous to themselves or to others or if they were so grievously disabled as not to be able to care for themselves I kept them in commitment. I appointed lawyers for them if they desired further hearings or wished to appeal my rulings.

I recall no reversals.

I still see and hear those disturbed people in dreams and, now and then, in fact.

Before I was circuit judge I represented people accused of crimes; when I was prosecutor I tried hard to convict the accused; when I was in the legislature I sometimes tried changing the laws that affected the accused.

I wrote about all that in my books and still do.

Now my loved wife lies in a nursing home suffering from Parkinson's. She has dementia and she sees people long dead plus the ghost of our first boy child. She has lost more than twenty percent of her weight and she is frail, but is now more beautiful than she was at nineteen to me.

She cries at times. She is bewildered and confused and sometimes knows no one including me. I cry with her and for her and for myself. I wish without hope that I could take her sickness and make it mine and give her back the life she so enjoyed and was so good at living.

I am doing book twenty-two now and it goes slowly. It works as *Robak in Black* and my protagonist is both a judge and my aging friend, Don Robak. His wife suffers from a condition caused by the actions of those who hate Robak. These enemies gave her a disease and she almost died and now remains lost. Her disease is much like Parkinson's and so I steal from what I see, the tears of my wife and the smells and sights and deaths in the crowded nursing home that is like a hive around her now.

And I write about all this although sometimes I must cry in the midst of the writing.

Sometimes it hurts.

I am no longer a sailor or Marine, no longer a legislator, prosecutor, judge, or even lawyer.

But for whatever life is worth I hope I am still a writer.

(Charlotte Hensley died June 10, 2000.)

Paint Doctor

The letter arrived at Henderson's law office on a dull, fall day. It was a substantial letter covered with bright, Japanese stamps. Sam Henderson took it from his secretary. When she was gone he opened the letter and found one sheet of paper inside folded around another sealed envelope. The second envelope was marked: *To be opened when I die,* then signed, *Iwo.* Henderson hefted it, tempted a little because he was and always had been a curious man and because he'd not heard from Iwo for a long time. He regretfully, finally, put it aside.

The single sheet contained only a few lines:

Paint Doctor,

I write you from a hospital. People look at me and we smile, but I know I am sick. Should I die, you may then read the letter I enclose herewith. My family and hopefully some part of my countrymen join me in thanking you for the years of life you gave me.

Iwo

Henderson read the note several times, examined the sealed envelope once more, held it up to the light, but could make nothing out, then put it in a drawer and locked it there.

He sat back in his chair, remembering, thinking back to an old, almost forgotten war.

★ ★ ★ ★ ★

It had been almost a lifetime since Henderson had first seen Iwo, Colonel Iwo.

Then, Henderson had been a Chief Pharmacist flown to Santuck Island on a PBY seaplane to replace an independent duty corpsman who'd come down with Filariasis, so that everything south of his navel had suddenly swollen to alarming size. The plane flew Henderson in and the anonymous corpsman out on the same flight from and to Guam.

Henderson found himself being welcomed, if that was the appropriate word, in the steaming heat of a bomb-damaged concrete wharf by three marines—a captain, a gunny sergeant, and a corporal.

"Get the new Chief's seabag, Corporal King," the captain ordered crisply. He received Henderson's salute and wiped ineffectually at his sweaty forehead in return. "It's cooler here after dark," he apologized. "I'm Captain Azus." He indicated the gunny sergeant. "Sergeant Donnelly." He gave Henderson an intent, appraising look. "The General asked them to send someone who could play bridge. Do you play bridge?"

"I'd be rusty," Henderson said.

Sergeant Donnelly smiled. "If you can count honor points, you're a better man than the inept lad you replaced."

Henderson examined the three marines. They all looked tough, competent, and battle proven. "Third Division?"

Captain Azus nodded. "Sure. Real Jap eaters. Come on now. We'll show you your quarters and you can get settled in, Chief. The prisoners will be with you for sick call at eight in the morning. There are some things General Kershand will want you to know about our routine before then."

"Routine?" Henderson asked, not understanding.

"Yes. There's this program the General has set up. Your

11

part in it is that if a prisoner complains of hurting outside then you paint the sore spot with merthiolate. If he hurts inside you give him two A.P.C.'s. That's all."

"Someone could die," Henderson said uncertainly, not liking the instructions.

"Several of our people did," Sergeant Donnelly said, still smiling, but not so much now. "Eleven of them. We believe they were mostly downed fliers. Maybe there'd have been a survivor or two off a tin can that went down six months ago in the narrows. We think the prisoners you'll be treating under our orders killed those eleven." He nodded. "General Kershand doesn't want things made easy for them. And we think they're healthy enough. They get lots of sun and exercise." He smiled once more, this time without humor.

"You mean they killed our people during the war?"

"Not exactly. Say, instead, right at the end of it, executed them, Samurai sword stuff. All the bodies were found in a common grave inside the prisoners' compound. Without their heads. We're still looking for the heads." Donnelly nodded seriously. "Every time we get even a hint about those heads I go dig another hole. It's become a game. I've maybe dug fifty holes so far without success."

"I see."

"The Japs you'll be treating are the prime murder suspects, Colonel Iwo and his four top aides. Some people don't think we can break them. We think we can. We think we can get enough on them to hang them all. Our methods are our business. General Kershand wants nothing to interfere." He nodded. "God help you if you get in the way, Chief."

Henderson had two large tents, both with raised plywood floors. One was a hospital tent, the other, situated behind it, was for storage and sleeping. The hospital tent was well equipped for a corpsman on independent duty without a medical officer. There was a complete pharmacy, an autoclave, surgical instruments, and even a small, portable X-ray machine.

He settled in. He was twenty-eight years old and his enlistment would end in December. His course was set: He'd go back to the States for one final year of law school. But first there'd be a few months of Santuck Island to endure.

Don't rock the boat, he told himself.

He began to unload his seabag. He put extra socks, skivvies, and khakis in an empty locker. Up the way, through a net window, he could see the marine encampment. It wasn't very large. Beyond that there would be the tents of the surrendered Japanese, thousands of them.

Henderson made himself be only mildly curious about Santuck Island. Since Guadalcanal he'd seen a dozen islands. Now he was tired of islands and atolls, glad the war was done, ready to go home. He'd seen good men die, young, bright men. Five Japanese prisoners meant little to him. He told himself he was only mildly curious about them because he'd be treating them.

He went through the marine chow line and stoically ate what they gave him. He then returned to his tents, unpacked the rest of his gear; and the few tattered law books he'd carried for almost four years.

When darkness came the marines came to his tent.

There were three of them again, Captain Azus, Sergeant Donnelly, and one new one. They came into the light of his tent, closing the screen quickly behind them against the darting, whirring night moths. They stomped and smiled.

"Get the cards," Azus said. "They're in that drawer." He pointed. He nodded at the man Henderson had not seen before. "This here's General Kershand."

Henderson snapped to attention.

"You needn't do that, son," the one star General said gently. "I read your records this afternoon. You were at the Canal with the First Divisions like me and Azus and Donnelly. You probably hate Japs as bad as we do." He stepped into the light. His hair was white and cut very short. He was thin and small and old, but he exuded energy. Henderson knew of him. A tough man. Mean.

There couldn't be more than a few hundred marines on Santuck Island. Not enough for a General to command. Henderson had a moment of intuition.

"The prisoners?" he asked. "You're here because of them?"

General Kershand took no offense. "I know the Japanese. I know how to deal with them. So I was sent." He smiled. "Long days. A lot of questions, but not enough answers yet. So get the cards and let's play bridge. A tenth of a cent a point. I'll take your part if you don't trust yourself to gamble. The last corpsman didn't."

"I'll gamble."

General Kershand nodded approvingly at him. "Show him what we brought, Donnelly."

Donnelly handed Henderson a small sack. Inside there were a dozen eggs, a loaf of bread, and a quarter pound of butter.

"Put those in your reefer. After three rubbers we'll cook them up on your hotplate." He gave Henderson a grin. "The General gets you. Captain Azus and I are partners from way back."

Henderson nodded. A square table was pushed into the circle of light. The cards were dealt.

Henderson was at first nervous and cautious. He soon found that none of the other three were truly expert bridge

14

players. They all three played similarly, wide open, psych bids, doubles and redoubles, daring leads, very cutthroat. Of the three, General Kershand was the most daring, the most unorthodox.

Henderson adapted. He had, in undergraduate and law school, played duplicate and regular contract bridge with able players. For a long time he'd teamed with a sarcastic man who was a life master and very good. The man, in their partnership, had incessantly smoked black cigars, used foul language, and been completely intolerant of error. Henderson was rusty, but the game soon returned, in all its intricacies, to him.

With only fair cards he and the General whomped the other two. Four dollars plus apiece.

Over eggs and toast running with butter Henderson asked diffidently, "I'd like to hear more about the island."

"Why?" General Kershand asked.

"Curiosity. And I have to treat the prisoners."

The General held up a warning hand. "Stay shy of it, Chief. They had no mercy for our people and now must be shown none in return. You will treat them within my rules. Soon, when there's a bit more evidence, our legal people will come in, relieve me, then fly them back to Japan for trial."

"Yes, sir. I see," Henderson said, not seeing at all.

"We've a dozen Japanese soldiers who'll testify to seeing Iwo and the rest enter into the prisoner compound the day after Hiroshima. We've got statements from two enlisted Koreans who dug the burial hole that morning. We can't yet put Samurai swords in the prisoners' hands. But one of them will break, one of the five. I know the Japs. One will want to live."

"The heads are the peculiar thing," Captain Azus said. His face was shadowed, out of the light. "No one but those

15

five can tell us where the heads went. But soon, with luck, we'll know that also. If we had the heads, we might be able to identify the victims individually through service dental charts. We know you were in law school, and so you know it could make for an easier trial."

The General frowned at Henderson. "Forget your law school for now. Remember only that this is our business and particularly my business, son. You paint them and pill them. Anything more has to clear through me, and *it won't*. It's my job to make their lives intolerable until one of them breaks. We'll run them, grill them, run them some more. Not much sleep and not much food. And then they have the added burden of Iwo."

"What about Iwo?" Henderson dared to ask.

"You'll soon see." The General scraped at the rest of his eggs. "It's you and me against these two young bandits from now on. You're a cautious player, but a good one."

He gave Henderson an approving look. "Take more chances."

In the morning Henderson found out about Iwo. Two battle-garbed guards escorted four trotting prisoners, all of the procession quick stepping along. The four prisoners were slowed because they carried a stretcher. The fifth prisoner rested on the stretcher.

Outside the guards lined the sweaty prisoners up. One marine stayed on guard. The other brought the prisoners in, one by one.

The Japanese were short, dour men. They looked tired, ill at ease, stretched to the breaking point. They smelled of fish and sweat and dirt. None of the four who'd borne the stretcher spoke English. All had nicknames given them by the guards.

"This one's called Squirrel," the guard intoned. "The last doc always gave him two A.P.C.'s."

Henderson nodded and obeyed his instructions. He pilled two, Squirrel and Ace, then painted two, Eddie and Wing.

"You'll have to come outside for the other one," the guard said apologetically. "He won't get up so the others have to carry him." He winked. "I think it's getting to the place where they're damned tired of it."

Henderson went outside. The fifth man lay in the stretcher smiling a little, looking up at the hot blue sky.

"New doctor," he said conversationally.

"I'm Chief Henderson. You must be Colonel Iwo."

"No talking to him," one of the guards warned harshly. "He can talk to you, but the rules are you say nothing back."

Henderson nodded.

Iwo smiled even more. One thin hand unbuttoned a faded shirt, very dirty, devoid of any insignia of rank. His chest, on both sides, was painted red.

"Hurt chest," he explained. "Air raid. Your flying bastards."

Henderson bent forward to inspect. The smell made him almost gag. Iwo was gaunt and each bone showed. There was a peculiar, small lump on the right side at collarbone level. Henderson touched it gently.

"Paint me," Iwo commanded softly. "Paint me, doctor. Do your part in this slow ritual you make us die by."

Henderson hesitated and then dutifully painted fresh merthiolate over the man's upper chest. When he was done, at command, the other four, Squirrel, Ace, Eddie, and Wing hoisted Iwo and began their trot back to their compound. The trailing guard lifted his rifle to Henderson and grinned.

"Thanks, Doc. See you tomorrow."

★ ★ ★ ★ ★

Henderson adopted a routine. Each morning, first off, he would solemnly attend to the prisoners, never varying their treatment. Later in the day he'd hold sick-call hours for the marines. There he could use his considerable medical skills. He treated everything from persistent ear fungus and heat rashes to occasional broken bones. Only when something seemed beyond him did he consign a patient to the daily Guam plane and the hospital there.

Once, years before, Henderson had complained when the Navy sent him to hospital corps school, ignoring his legal background. It had done no good. So, that failing, he'd become expert, made the Navy way his way, and survived.

After sick call he'd loll the rest of the day away, reading books from the small camp library, or studying his few precious law books.

At nights, almost every night, he played bridge with the same foursome. To the great delight of General Kershand, despite the fact that Henderson continued to play his conservative game, he and Henderson won consistently.

Henderson would have been content except for the prisoners. It made him feel unsure participating in a nullity.

"Why do the guards bring the prisoners at all?" he inquired after a game one night.

Captain Azus answered. "Geneva Convention, Chief. Prisoners are entitled to medical attention." He smiled. "The Japs winked at it. We've learned what we're doing here from the enemy. Cruelty brings cruelty. So medical attention means what we decide, not what they expect and want."

"The war's over," Henderson said reasonably.

"Not yet. Not for those who did what was done here."

Henderson shook his head. "It worries me. I think there may really be something wrong with Colonel Iwo."

General Kershand shook his head. "He's faking and the others are helping him. That's why we make them carry him with them every place they go. Iwo presented his sword to me at the surrender, all very correct and ceremonial then. When the bodies were found he took to bed."

"I'd like to X-ray him," Henderson said.

General Kershand shook his head. "No way."

"If you ordered it and I found nothing, then that could hurt him at a future trial."

"I won't change the way we're doing things. One of those men will break if things continue as they are now. We run them and question them. They only sleep two hours at a stretch. Then we start on them again. Stop being a lawyer." He shook his head. "No way."

In deep night, soon after, there came to be a way. Henderson was shaken awake by Captain Azus.

"Come with me, Henderson. Now! There's hell to pay."

Henderson pulled on rumpled khakis and got into the captain's Jeep. They jolted down a rusty road at an excessive speed and parked near a small, barbed-wire enclosure. Flashlights picked them up, beckoned them on.

"This way. This way."

Four prisoners, Squirrel, Ace, Eddie, and Wing, lay bloodily dead in a large single tent in the center of the enclosure. The fifth prisoner, Colonel Iwo, bled sluggishly from his wrists. Henderson ignored the dead and examined Iwo. The cuts were straight, but not, hopefully, deep enough.

"They all cut their wrists," Azus said, somehow scandalized about it. "God knows where they got a razor. We check them all the time. They passed it on, one to another. Iwo was last. Maybe he chickened out. The others cut groins too. He didn't."

"Get him to my tent. I'll sew him up and start plasma," Henderson said. "He's lost a lot of blood. He's weak and could die also."

Captain Azus nodded agreement. "The General isn't going to be happy about this. A lot of us are going to catch hell."

Henderson directed the shaken guards in loading Iwo into the jeep. He kept pressure on the wrist cuts, stopping the bleeding. Iwo sat in the seat with his head back, looking up curiously at the night sky, his eyes open.

"Paint doctor," he said softly. "Damn paint doctor. Let me die. Then all this will be done."

"No," Henderson said firmly.

In the tent he sewed the cuts together and gave Iwo plasma, one unit, then another. When blood pressure and pulse were more normal he wheeled the X-ray unit into place and X-rayed Iwo's chest. The guards watched curiously, making no protests.

General Kershand stomped angrily in as Henderson was reading the wet film.

"Four dead men," he said savagely. "This bastard the only one left." He shook his head. "And I find you violating my express orders."

"Yes, sir. I'm sorry, sir. Could I ask you if when he surrendered his sword to you at the ceremony did he make a big thing out of it? Did he draw it, flourish it, lift it, swing it?"

"He gave it to me. That's all." The General shook his white head. "I'd put you in the brig if I had anyone else to treat this murdering Jap. I may do that yet."

"Yes, sir," Henderson continued. "I was wrong, but the pain for him must have been excruciating." He pointed at the X-ray. "His collarbone's splintered on the right side. You can see the break and the calcification around it. The edges don't meet well. If he tried doing much, even now, he might cause the fracture to compound, come through the skin. And there are, at my count, at least four rib fractures on his left side, probably more. Our last bombing raid on Santuck—was it before or after Hiroshima?"

"I'd guess before. After the bomb at Hiroshima everything stopped in this area." General Kershand drew closer to the X-ray film, frowning at it.

"This man didn't cut off any heads with that shoulder."

"This is none of your affair," General Kershand said coldly. "This man is your enemy. You're not his lawyer. Whether he wielded a sword or not, he was in command of this island. He participated."

"General, with all respect, this man will eventually be tried by lawyers, defended by other lawyers. Without someone around to put the sword in his hand or the words of command in his mouth, he's not going to be found guilty."

"Perhaps. That's conjecture."

Henderson nodded surely.

"They've beaten me, then," General Kershand said softly. "They died to beat me."

Henderson sensed the same thing. He nodded.

The General looked away and then back. He smiled sourly. "My recollection is you're due out in December, Henderson. You've probably cost yourself some added time tonight. With four dead and Colonel Iwo in the shape he's in, my job here's done. I'm going to fly back to Guam with you and Iwo." He stopped for a moment, thinking. "Maybe there'll be a decent bridge game there for an old plunger who's about to retire." He nodded. "You argue Iwo's case with the legal people there. You show your X-rays to the doctors."

"Yes, sir," Henderson said.

"Why, Henderson? Why bother with an animal like him?"

Henderson thought for a moment. "Perhaps because what we were doing was no more right than what Colonel Iwo was accused of doing. Also, because I was curious. Mostly because he tried hard to die with the others, to cheat us also. His cuts are straight. There are no hesitation marks. He just couldn't get pressure enough on the blade to get the job done. He was so weak he never got to his groin area. Maybe the razor was dull. But if he couldn't commit suicide, he logically couldn't lop off heads with a Samurai sword."

The man on the cot moaned. They both watched as he awoke and stared about him. He pulled weakly at the bandages on his wrists, but they were secure.

"Paint doctor," he called. "Damn paint doctor."

"More than that," General Kershand said. He shook his head and went out into the night.

The obituary made the front page. It recounted Iwo's accomplishments as a Japanese statesman, as a leader of the diet or legislature, as a cabinet member. The story said the sane world had lost a sane, reliable friend. There was even, Henderson found, a long, complimentary, even flowery, editorial about Iwo inside.

Henderson unlocked the drawer and opened the second letter:

Dear Paint Doctor,

What I did, during the war years, seemed right to me then. Things I did then are abhorrent to me now. Thank you for helping me. What your people did to me and the others attempting to obtain our confessions was also a wrong. I am glad I did not die. Perhaps I am now innocent as once I was guilty.

One of your prisoners, the last one, broke my collarbone. The rib injuries did occur during an earlier air raid.

My family died at Hiroshima. With strong drugs and hot anger all things become possible. When it was over I alone weighted the sack of heads and dropped them secretly in Santuck Bay.

Iwo

Henderson read the letter without surprise or regret. He put it back in the drawer when he was finished. A few days later he remembered it, took it out, read it once more, then burned it.

Deadly Hunger

They were, Bruno found, people of anger and violence, particularly Aunt Nora. They were thumpers, pinchers, beaters, living in singly held camps, sometimes together, but apart in many ways.

Ralph was mean and lazy. Aunt Nora was mean and penurious.

Watching the two of them made Bruno feel a little like he'd felt the night he'd been thrown a hundred, skidding feet from the auto crash which had burned his mother to death: unable to move, fascinated and horrified at what he must see.

If he placed an empty glass against the bedroom wall, he could hear them when they weren't running the old, window air-conditioner. He was afraid to do it often because it was an uncertain summer weatherwise. Besides, Aunt Nora could move very silently.

He heard Aunt Nora say once, "He's so damned much trouble, rolling here, rolling there. He's started eating a lot, too. Have you noticed? I should go to court for more money, but that might mean trouble." She paused and Bruno had to strain to hear. "There's his trust fund. More than a quarter million."

Ralph, out-of-work actor, husband number three for Nora, said something, but Bruno missed it. He talked softly, was huge, and now and then he'd pinch Bruno or thump him on the head, but usually he ignored him. Aunt Nora was the one to fear.

"I'll think of something," Aunt Nora said.

★ ★ ★ ★ ★

Bruno was twelve years old that summer when Aunt Nora came to take him home from the LaRuse Home and School.

"I'd like to stay here," he told her truthfully. "I like it okay, Aunt Nora." He'd called her that grudgingly, because the social worker had said he should. "There's a pool and a gym. The doctor said if I worked hard there's an outside chance for me to walk in braces one day."

She smiled an unbelieving, false-teeth smile at him. She was his great aunt, old, and his only living relative. He remembered his mother hadn't liked her and they'd never visited.

"I talked to welfare and they went to the judge and he gave you to me." She gave him a severe look. "You need to be realistic, young man. Paraplegics don't outgrow it." She nodded. "I'm going to take you. There's only Ralph and me. I'm semi-retired from pictures. We have a nice place."

Miss Malvin, the social worker who supervised the home, nodded at both of them, her puckered face eager. Bruno was sure Miss Malvin would be glad to be rid of him. He was the only wheelchairer in the school. He'd tried not to be a problem, but by the very nature of his disablement, knew he had been.

"Bruno's self-sufficient," she said. "Give him a problem and he's very dogged and determined about it. He'll solve it every time."

Aunt Nora nodded, watching him, her small, steely eyes unreadable. Bruno tried to remember what Mom had said about her. She'd been an actress, a medium successful one, a character actress. That was where she'd met Ralph, her present husband. He was in pictures or on the stage or something. Bruno remembered Mom had shown him a squib about the marriage in the newspaper.

"He's a thinker, a planner, and a doer," Miss Malvin said. "Even boys in here for delinquency respect and get along with Bruno."

Bruno smiled. What Miss Malvin said was true. He'd waited until the largest and meanest of the bully boys was asleep and whaled him good with a two-by-four. Bruno's legs might be gone, but his arms were very strong. Now the mean ones in the school mostly let him alone. He was unpredictable. There was easier prey.

"He gets Social Security," Miss Malvin continued. "We'll have that transferred to you."

"Isn't there some sort of trust fund?" Aunt Nora asked, smiling some more, playing the kindly interested aunt. "How's that handled?"

"Now it just builds with interest and dividends. Someday Bruno will be a wealthy boy. The Social Security's enough to pay for him here." Miss Malvin nodded her head. "The trust is quite large."

"How large?" Aunt Nora asked.

Miss Malvin frowned a little, but then wrote a number on a pad and turned it so only she and Aunt Nora could read it. Bruno knew what was in the trust, so he didn't care.

"Who has the money?"

"First National," Miss Malvin said. "Everything in it is subject to court audit."

"I see," Aunt Nora said. She smiled and nodded and watched Bruno and, once again, he couldn't read her eyes.

"Home" turned out to be a hot, small room in an old house in the center of a fenced-in quarter block. The house was tree shaded, with rutted walks, plus an old shed in the back yard. The house was in the middle of a decaying neighborhood. It was turn-of-the-century built and needed paint and cleaning. The inside walls of the house were covered with photos and clippings about a younger Aunt Nora, usually in costume, mostly taken with men. In a few pictures Bruno could also recognize Ralph, a hundred pounds lighter, thirty years younger.

"Home" quickly became Aunt Nora constantly ordering and punishing Bruno. She was better at punishments than the people at the school. She had imagination. She washed his mouth out with a blistering soap, when he cursed, she beat his hands with her shoe when his bed was unmade. When he did badly she punished him. When he did well she demanded better and punished him again.

She was a woman born to command. She refused to lose any argument. Ralph was twice her size, but Bruno soon knew Nora ran the house.

She was also stingy, a collector of used twine, paper, aluminum cans, returnable bottles, and anything else with resale value. She counted her pennies constantly and begrudged every one she spent.

Bruno moped badly at first, lonesome for the school and the few friends he'd made there. He skipped meals and picked at those he didn't skip. Neither Aunt Nora nor Ralph seemed to notice.

It was dog days summer. School was not yet in session, there was no place for Bruno to go, nothing to do. Daytime television he found incredibly stupid. Nora and Ralph watched it avidly, commenting on how good it was, sometimes playing the soap opera parts themselves.

Bruno willed himself to survive. He'd done it before, when his mother died, when he'd found out he was bound to a wheelchair. He began to eat to regain lost strength, he started exercising his arms again. As much as he could he explored his new home, sometimes secretly abandoning the wheelchair, because it left telltale marks on the rug, and crawling to something he wanted, but might not be supposed, to see. He rolled his wheelchair here and there about the house so vigorously that Aunt Nora, exasperated, ordered Ralph to build a ramp down to the yard. When it was finished she forbade Bruno to leave the yard and then let him stay outside in it all day, if he wanted. Sometimes he imagined he could see her watching him in the shadows behind the windows, her face lost in darkness. Sometimes he thought Ralph watched also.

At times Bruno thought they hated each other. Other times he wasn't sure. They had similar interests. They acted things together other than the soaps. Sometimes he was Rhett, gallant and charming, and she was a peppery Scarlett. Sometimes she was Stanwyck and he was Cooper, sometimes he Bogart and she someone in trouble.

A lot of the time they were themselves. That was when Bruno had to watch and take care.

The yard was more interesting and safer than the house. There were two smaller lots adjoining behind the back fence. The inner lot had ramshackle apartments squeezed tightly on it. Black people and white people lived in the apartments and things were loud and violent on weekends.

The corner lot had a small single-family house and a tiny swimming pool behind it. He fell in love with the pool the first time he saw it. A thin, black lady came out and swam in it now and then. No one else seemed to use it. The thin lady had two dogs she always brought with her. She tied their leashes to the diving board post and swam while they lay panting in the shadows cast by the board. Bruno watched, polite, but envious. After a time the woman also noticed him. On the third day as he watched she unleashed her dogs and walked them his way.

"Hello," she said, holding the dogs back from the fence.

28

"Hello," Bruno said. He moved his wheelchair closer to the fence. "Is that your swimming pool?"

She smiled, exhibiting a lot of gold in white teeth. "I guess maybe. My mamma gave it to me when she died last year."

"Could I maybe swim in it sometime? I'm a very good swimmer, but I haven't had a chance for a while."

"You're forward," she said, but she was still smiling.

"Yes, ma'am, I guess I am. But I sure do like to swim."

She considered him. "Are you related to Nora Hubler? Or has God been good and she's moved on?"

"I'm her great nephew."

"That's too bad. I don't like her and she don't like me. You can bet she won't let you swim in my pool. I had some trouble with my husband and she stuck her nose in that. He died. She stuck it into that too. She calls the police on me anonymous every time she gets a chance." She nodded. "I used to have three dogs. One of them got over the fence and now there's only two. She put poison out in your yard. Disguised it in hamburger. She got it out of your little shed over there." She pointed. "Strychnine it was. Mean and quick. I sneaked over the fence one night and found a can of it after my dog died. I called the police about it, but they never sent anyone. I've got a reputation I guess. I got sent to a sanitarium instead of prison after my husband died. The local police didn't like that." She shook her head. "I guess I'd let you swim, all things considered. I'd have to be there to make sure you wasn't going to get drowned, 'cause I'd get blamed. But Nora won't let you. You ask and you'll see." She smiled without humor. "She needs bad to die. 'The Actress.' That's what she fancies herself." She watched Bruno through the fence. Her eyes were odd, out of focus. There'd been a boy in the school with eyes like hers, a crazy boy. He'd finally run away and been caught and sent to an asylum.

"My yard's very cramped for my puppies."

"They seem nice," Bruno said. They were huge brutes. They sat eyeing him like he was dinner, tongues lolling. Bruno was unafraid. He liked dogs.

"You do pretty good rolling that chair," the woman said.

Bruno smiled at her.

"Watch close back there by the corner of the shed. There's an old well. It's covered over, but some of the boards could be rotten."

Bruno nodded. Aunt Nora hadn't told him about any covered-over well, and he'd rolled over or close to it a dozen times. *That was funny.*

"What's your name?" he asked the pool lady.

"Call me Miss June," she said, staring down at him. "Your dear auntie calls me Crazy June. The police do, too. But being thought crazy sometimes has its compensations."

Bruno couldn't think of any.

Miss June was right about one thing, though. When Bruno asked Aunt Nora about using the pool she flew into a cold, two-day whipping rage, à la Davis and Crawford.

A few days later the food war started. All that day, earlier, Aunt Nora had been very silent. She'd had her account books out, totaling figures, checking the amounts in her various accounts, frowning a lot.

She'd called Bruno in one time.

"I may need to go to court and get appointed guardian of your trust fund," she said, watching him. "Would you help?"

Somehow he knew, if he did, it would all continue on as it was now.

"I'd like to go back to the LaRuse Home," he said.

She nodded, as if deciding something. Later that day,

without reason, she stalked him and smacked him three different times.

At dinner that night she called fat Ralph a hog.

Dinner had been spotty, a tiny bread and cracker crumb extended meat loaf, some limp lima beans, and a gelatine dessert. When it was done and she was clearing the table Ralph stayed seated and ordered her to bring him bread and peanut butter and jelly which he loved.

"You've had a God's plenty," she said, exasperated.

"I'm fully grown," he said, "twice your size, little woman. I need more to eat." His voice was sweet and reasonable.

"Get out and rustle yourself up a job then. Forget the studios. Take anything. Then put something more in the pot."

"I've still got ten more weeks of unemployment left. You take the check for that every week." He waved a table knife in the air. "I want more food."

"From this day you'll eat what I eat, nothing more, nothing less." She turned to Bruno and he knew part of her performance was also for him. "Same goes for you. Eating machines, the both of you. Food costs a lot of money."

And so hostilities began in what Bruno found to be a genteel, but bitter war in which he soon discovered he was the main casualty. Breakfast became a piece of dry toast, an apple, and sweet coffee, which Nora loved. Lunch was a sandwich or a single bowl of thin soup. Supper was stringy, cheap meat, a vegetable, and water to drink.

Ralph smiled and ate the meals without complaint. He seemed big enough to take what he wanted from the kitchen shelves by force, but he didn't.

After a few days of privation Bruno found Ralph had employed other strategies.

Aunt Nora said, "Your check didn't come today from the unemployment."

31

Ralph smiled mockingly. "Maybe it'll come tomorrow." He nodded slyly. "You watch close for it, Nora."

She shook her head suspiciously.

"It better had. You'll eat nothing else—in this house until I get that check. And you'll not use my car, either."

"I got to eat, Nora," Ralph whined. He patted his ponderous belly. "Without your car I can't go around to the studios and to my agent and I can't sign up for unemployment." He sat very straight in his chair, anger growing, getting redder and redder in the face until Bruno thought he might pop. "I got me a box at the post office. My check goes there now."

Nora nodded coldly. "Bring it here and eat here again."

Bruno had a premonition of personal disaster. He rolled a little back from the table, watching both of them, wondering whether this was a game or for real.

Ralph said, "If I don't eat then neither of you eat. I'll stay in our house and wait you out, Nora." He gave Bruno a venomous look. "That goes for the kid, too. He could go with you to court and then there'd be plenty of money. So it's his fault and your fault." He tapped his belly again. "I'll live off fat. You two won't last long." He looked at both of them hard, in what he sometimes called his George Raft style.

Aunt Nora smiled some then and Ralph finally smiled back.

"It's his fault," Aunt Nora said, nodding at Bruno accusingly. "I agree that's it. But I'll make do, Ralph."

"Sure you will," he said, lightly enough. "So will I. So be it."

Later, Bruno saw Ralph move out of the joint bedroom to the living room couch. From there he could patrol Nora's kitchen.

That night, while he lay awake and thought, Bruno could hear Ralph moving restlessly about the house, pausing here

32

and there. Sometimes Bruno fancied he could hear the kitchen cabinet doors open and shut quietly. Finally there was silence, then snoring.

The next morning Aunt Nora confided, "He won't find anything in the kitchen. I hid the edibles in my closet when his check didn't come."

She brought him a single apple for the first missed meal and watched grudgingly as he ate it.

"You could end this," she said. "Go with me to court."

He almost agreed. Then, he shook his head. "I'd like to go back to the school."

After that food got *very* sparse.

Experimenting, Bruno found the best place to listen. In the stillness of his room, glass pressed to wall, he imagined he could hear her eating at night, her false teeth clicking.

On the second day she brought him some milk, a whole small container.

"Boys need milk," she said, not looking directly at him. She patted him gingerly on the head, doing the good mother bit. When she left he tried the milk. It was sour.

On the third day there was a single, brown banana.

He'd looked for Miss June before, but she'd been gone. On that third day he saw her in her pool. He rolled down the ramp. Aunt Nora was having her nap and Ralph sat on the couch watching him sourly as he rolled past.

He told Miss June. His stomach ached from hunger. He felt hot and weak.

Ralph had vanished from the house for several hours that morning before retaking possession of the couch.

"He's got a whole sack of groceries, mostly peanut butter and jelly and bread, behind his couch now," Bruno whispered. "And she's got stuff in her closet."

"You poor kid," Miss June said. "I could maybe call that

home or welcome for you anonymous like if you'd want. Maybe they'd come out and check, maybe not." She shook her head and water flew from her swim cap. Her two dogs panted and eyed Bruno like an old bone. "That might stop them. This time, anyway. Or you could tell your aunt you're ready to go to court with her and then tell the judge what they're doing."

Bruno shook his head. Aunt Nora would know.

"How about the lady that ran the home where you were?"

Bruno remembered Miss Malvin. Aunt Nora had a court order. Miss Malvin worshipped court orders. Besides, Aunt Nora was feeding him *some,* wasn't she. He shook his head again. Mom's trial, where he'd gotten the money, had taught him the law was slow and unpredictable. The school had taught him that kids died. He'd heard a thousand horror stories, most of them true.

"I don't have my money yet," he said. "Someday I will have it. A lot of money." He nodded at Miss June and tried to work his way through the current insanity, forcing himself to be logical. "Could you loan me some food? Someday I'll pay it back."

Miss June nodded. "I can get you some, but remember it'll be a one-time shot. If I go in and get it now, she'll take away your ramp and you'll not get back outside again." She gave him a wise look. "She's a careful woman, your Aunt Nora. She wants everything to look right. Little and thin as you are she maybe believes you'll get sick and die and then she'll get all your money. Then their problem, if it's real, would be over. But I've always heard she had money. I'll bet there isn't even a problem."

Bruno had considered that before. He'd tried to find and look at her account books, but she kept them under lock and key. He considered it again.

Were they laughing at him, playing their hunger act with him as pawn? They were both eating. They weren't hot and sick and weak.

If he got sick and died she could just say he wouldn't eat. She'd have Miss Malvin testify he'd not wanted to leave the home. She could say things like he was despondent, that he'd refused food, become ill. She could tell them she'd just not realized how sick he was. And who'd worry about or believe anything Crazy June said?

"First things first," Miss June said. "I'll smuggle you something out behind the shed tonight. When you come out tomorrow eat it out of sight and maybe she won't know."

He nodded. Aunt Nora would know—if not tomorrow, then the day after or the day after that. He thought some more. He didn't like life much living in a wheelchair, but the idea of dying was worse. He remembered what dying had been like for Mom. It had been heat, screams, pain.

If he survived this time then wouldn't Ralph and Nora invent another time?

Tonight he'd stay awake and listen.

Tomorrow was Nora's habitual store day.

He already knew where Ralph's cache of food was. Aunt Nora's was someplace in her room, probably in the closet, just like she'd said.

He could crawl into her bedroom so there'd be no telltale wheelchair marks on her rug.

She'd eat the oldest food first. That was her parsimonious way. And drink sweet, black coffee.

Ralph could be harmless without her, but perhaps not. Bruno looked toward the house and wondered if they were watching him. Maybe they were laughing at him right now, awarding each other Oscars.

Ralph too, then.

"You'd like your dogs to run over here in the yard again?" he asked Crazy June.

"Sure," she said, eyes sparkling. "Just like you'd like to swim in my pool."

He nodded and let his head hang down limply in the event they were watching.

"In a moment, Miss June, you shake your head at me. Act like you're angry and saying no to me. And then a big favor: They'd see me if I went in the shed, but when you set the food out tonight, could you go into the shed and get some of the strychnine Aunt Nora gave your dog?"

She watched him, her eyes crazy, but smiling.

"Is it quick and sure?" he asked.

"It was on Bobo." She smiled. "I'm going to be gone all day tomorrow with lots of people around so I don't get blamed." She smiled some more. "They won't ever think it's you. They'll think it's murder and suicide."

"Would a person taste it?" he persisted.

"I don't know. I don't want to know, but I've heard it's bitter. Mix it with something sweet, syrup, sugar." She watched him from a far-away place, and he smiled at her: "Then mix it with whatever."

Maybe Aunt Nora's sweet coffee? Ralph's jelly for his peanut butter sandwiches?

"A lot of it please," Bruno said, remembering Ralph's girth.

He wondered if they'd play a death scene.

Widow

She'd called and been sweet right after she filed for divorce. I could come any time that day and pick up my clothes. We could "talk," she said. I parked down the road out of sight and peeped under an improperly drawn shade. I could see her sitting in the shadowed front room of our tiny house. Her attitude was one of patient waiting. She was holding something I couldn't quite identify in her right hand. I rubbed the telephone wire in two.

I'm cautious. I've always been. Perhaps it comes out of my Scots ancestry, perhaps it's from seeing my parents burn in the accident where I was thrown clear. After that I lived with my grandparents, who'd as soon waste money as words. There was no one to run to. I was too small for competitive sports. I had some late growth and am of average height and weight now, but I suppose those early years made me more of a thinker and a planner than a doer. It seemed natural to me to want to be a lawyer. Caution has aided, not impeded, my practice.

I met Janice Willingham during my second year in a Bington law firm. I was the "associate" in the office. This meant mostly that when something piddling came up one of the two partners would come to my door and beckon imperiously. I did collections, unimportant damage suits, divorces, and minor criminal stuff. It was a start.

One partner said little to me and smiled condescendingly when I ventured an opinion. To the other, the world was a plural woman. All persons were "she." If Bill Jones came into the office while I was out, this partner would dutifully inform me "she'd" been in. Perhaps a result of femlib, perhaps something else. I wondered sometimes how that second partner had lived fifty-odd years without acquiring contusions enough to break the habit. The smiler was named Connell, the gender-confuser was Guyman. My name is Sam Hubbard.

On the day Janice Willingham first came into the office both partners were out, so I got her.

She was something. I think a few like her are born each generation just to make men and women alike recognize true physical perfection. She was a trim blonde, with eyes so deep and green you could fall in them and drown. Her figure made all the figures I'd seen before seem to be totally wrong. She was wearing a simple little dress. Later, I found out the dress had cost almost three hundred dollars.

Her voice, when it came, was untutored, but soft and feminine. She waited until the awed secretary had gone out.

"I wanted to see you about a divorce," she said.

"Sit down. Sit down." Her voice brought me back to being a lawyer. I opened my third drawer left. There, typed in bold face and taped to the bottom of the drawer, I kept a list of my state's requirements for obtaining a divorce. I thought I could now get by without the list, but this was a time of stress and I didn't trust myself completely.

"What's your name and when and where were you married?" I asked, to get her started.

Her story was old and trite. She'd married a man named True Willingham. I instantly recognized the name. The Willinghams owned the canning factory and controlled Bington's largest bank. I'd heard some about True. He was an indolent member of an industrious family. He'd never worked—factory or bank. He was much older than Janice, in his far fifties. She claimed he'd become increasingly jealous. Every glance at another person, every word she uttered was weighed and tested upon the scales of his colorful imagination.

She showed me bruises on her neck and arms from the night before. She complained he'd struck her on other occasions. When she'd threatened him with police he'd laughed at her. I was properly sympathetic and indignant.

"He told me last night maybe he'd kill me and then commit suicide," she said. A little tear came in the corner of her eye. "And he might. He's been drinking heavily. He hasn't been sober for days. I'm afraid of him."

True Willingham and family didn't worry me much. Our firm represented neither bank nor factory. I sent her to a photographer to have pictures taken of the bruises. Sometimes they come in handy in court.

I filed a divorce action for her.

All simple and routine. Except it wasn't. Not for her, and not for me, for different reasons.

All the time she was in my office I had this tremendous awareness of her. I thought she recognized it and perhaps used it. She needed me then.

On that day, after severing the telephone wire, I drove to the sheriff's office. Things must move. It was going on dusk. I wanted it dark.

"How about going out with me?" I asked Sheriff Bert Horn. "It'll be a quiet divorce. She told me to come pick up my clothes. You can be there to see there's no problem."

"Wait a minute," he said. "I'll call little Jannie and tell her we're on our way." He smiled, and I had a sudden bitter taste in my mouth.

He called, but of course there was no answer.

"Phone's probably out again," I said. "Let's take my car."

★ ★ ★ ★ ★

Two days after I first saw Janice, True Willingham was dead. His death caused a small furor before and after the grand jury finished its work. Poison deaths always do that.

I got the call from the sheriff's office at about three in the morning. I went right on down.

They had Janice in Sheriff Horn's kitchen. Horn was with her. A matron was pouring coffee. Janice sat in one of the straight chairs.

"You represent Mrs. Willingham?" handsome Sheriff Horn asked in the same voice that had helped him win election. I smiled at him. We were acquainted.

"Correct," I said cautiously.

Horn watched me. I could see he was testing the situation out. He said, "There's been some trouble. Did you file a divorce for Mrs. Willingham a few days ago?"

"I did. What kind of trouble?"

He held up a peremptory hand. "Let me ask the questions."

I smiled and shook my head. "Not with me, Sheriff Horn. Until I know what's going on you've gotten your last answer from me or my client if I'm still advising her."

A touch of color came into his face. "All right," he said testily. "True Willingham's dead. Mrs. Willingham tells us he called her to talk reconciliation. She visited his house. She admits they argued. She then says he knocked her around. She does have some bruises. Then he made her drink from a bottle of whiskey laced with strychnine, or thought he made her drink. He then *apparently* drank enough of it himself to kill three people."

I nodded. "They'd been having problems. I'll vouch for that. He threatened suicide."

I watched Janice. She sat carefully in Sheriff Horn's chair.

40

Her voice was low, "He gave up on beating me. I was back in a corner where he'd trapped me, just sort of sitting there. He kept cursing me, calling me unspeakable names, saying I'd be sorry. He had the whiskey bottle, and I knew he had something in it. He poured some in a glass for me and forced me to put it in my mouth, but I spit it out when I could, when he looked away. He drank a lot of it himself and then he fell down and rolled around. After a while he quit moving."

I went to her and held her and, after a while, as if she thought she ought to do it, she put her head on my shoulder and cried.

There were a few new bruises on her neck and arms. I thought I'd seen most of her bruises before, but I didn't say anything. When she'd quit crying I left her with the matron and went into the outer office and talked for a time with Bert Horn about it. He called the circuit judge and talked with him in low tones.

"I'm going to let her go for now," he said to me. He grinned familiarly at me before we went back to the kitchen to announce it. "To convict that lady of a crime she'd have to shoot a police officer or kill a kid, and the law would need the best evidence in the world and half women on the jury."

I never forgot the words.

We were married early the next spring and for a while it was fine. I bought us a handsome little cottage in the country a few miles from town. She wanted then to be away from people. There was some acreage with the cottage, and I taught her how to fish and together we learned how to shoot. She became a dead shot.

Although the grand jury had refused to indict her the town still talked. There was money and that didn't aid in stopping the malicious stories. True's will left it to her in trust with his bank as trustee. She couldn't abide that arrangement and so she nagged me into court and I got an order naming myself as trustee. The money wasn't a fortune, but it was enough to keep her comfortable for a long time, carefully used. True had been a member of a family with money, a great deal of it, but most of it was tied up in other trusts where True's interest terminated at death. Janice didn't like that either.

"He left me almost nothing," she said to me shortly before our marriage. She looked at me with those really great eyes. "Oh Sam, what would happen if I lost you?"

I was sentimentalist enough then not to tell her the correct answer. She'd find another man.

I said, "Maybe I could buy some more insurance."

She sniffed. "I've read about insurance."

I smiled. "Remember me? I'm the lawyer. In this state for you to not be paid off on insurance at my death you'd have to be convicted of my murder. True had no insurance. If he had, you'd have gotten it, assuming the policy named you as beneficiary."

She looked a little more enthusiastic.

For a wedding present I gave her a hundred-thousand-dollar term policy and spent a couple of hours with her going over the fine print. I had to dig sometimes to make the payments.

And so we were wed.

It wasn't a long time until she was unfaithful to me, only months from the date of our marriage.

Perhaps it would have worked for us if I'd had plenty of money, but I didn't have money. Young lawyers make a pittance. I was bright enough, but lawyers make money from time spent building a practice, from experience. I was coming along well enough in the office. Small victories had made the smiler begin to ask my opinion and the gender-confuser to nod approvingly. Once the latter even put his arm around my shoulder and announced to the smiler: "She's a good boy." The year we were married they put my name on the stationery and raised my pay.

The trouble was you couldn't buy very many three-hundred-dollar dresses on my salary. She'd come from a marriage with an adoring older man who could pay the bills to a youngster who couldn't. She ran through the trust income at high speed, always behind. She was a wild woman every time she got into a dress shop. I finally called a halt to that when she was spent six months ahead. I made her take something back. It was a cocktail dress, and it had cost more than two hundred dollars. I told her adamantly she'd have to return it and earned a look that contained only hate.

It was a bad marriage for me in many ways. She wasn't very intelligent. She had a kind of inquiring look of brightness that could pass for brains and fool her admirers, but the veneer was thin. She could make a mistake, be corrected, and then make the same mistake again. Other than with clothes she had the attention span of a six-year-old. She was intensely vain. I was something she used. In her mirror there was only a single reflection. She could waste a full day trying on clothes, standing in front of a mirror in rapt, silent contemplation. She was scrupulously neat with her person and her clothes. Other than that living with her was constant cleanup. She left a wake behind her, used glasses and dishes, crumpled, bright cigarettes.

I never stopped wanting her. She was so physically over-powering that I couldn't do that. It was only that I became more fully aware of her. It was like owning a beautiful expensive car. Only after you admired the sleek exterior did you notice that the motor wouldn't start.

As I said, I'm a cautious thinker. I'd pushed hard in school and achieved honors. I'd come to my small town of Bington for many reasons, not the least being an examination of longevity tables.

Marrying Janice was one of the few uncalculated things I'd done in my life. Sometimes I thought a part of me was standing away and shaking a finger at me even as we repeated our marriage vows.

When I was sure she was unfaithful I feigned a cold and moved into the second bedroom and waited and watched. The cerebral me was back in control.

I didn't have to wait long. The very next night she had the bottle out, a pretty party dress on, and wore a smile for me when I came home from the office.

"Cocktails and sin," she said.

I inspected her carefully. On her right arm there was a large, fresh bruise. "You've hurt yourself."

"Fell against a tree while I was outside target shooting." She held out her glass. "I'll fix you one."

"Better not," I said. "Cold's pretty bad and I'm taking pills you're not supposed to mix with liquor."

She looked forlorn and disappointed.

I tried not to look afraid.

I went on back to the second bedroom. I thought about killing her and knew I'd never manage it. I thought about her killing me and thought she probably would manage it. I thought also about the deceased True Willingham and the large insurance policy I'd bought his widow. Would she have the guts to try the same method she'd probably used on True? I remembered her making the same mistakes over and over.

I easily started an argument, then left the house.

Perhaps I could have stopped her desire to kill me by canceling the insurance policy, but I didn't do that.

44

The new man in her life was Sheriff Horn. I saw his car parked at the house several times.

It was full dark when we got to the house. No moon. I parked my car boldly in front. Then I led Horn up the path, staying out of the line of sight from the windows. On the porch I tapped on the door and then stepped quickly away from it.

"It's only me, Janice," I called, before Horn could say anything.

He was smiling when she began firing through the door. That *had* been a gun she was holding when I'd peeped through the windows.

I ran down the porch, vaulted the rail, and looked back. Horn was slumped against the door. He was making noises, but no words came. I wasn't sure how badly he was hit. He slid on down, and she put three more shots through the door. After the first one he didn't seem to notice.

I got back into my car and started it and waited. When nothing happened I put the car in gear and blew the horn. The door opened and she stood there looking down at Sheriff Horn. I noticed she was wearing a brand new dress—was it black?

I drove back to town, staying within all the speed laws. Both as a citizen and as an officer of the court it was now my duty to report a shooting.

A Lot of Sense

Gilbert Marnell was walking for exercise on a late Florida winter morning. Outside the wind chill temperature was in the low thirties so he walked in an enclosed mall south of Sarasota. The mall was crowded with invaders from the north, hordes of intent, red-eyed snowbirds.

Marnell literally ran into Joel Cassiday, unable to avoid the man without chancing a fall.

It had been ten years since he'd seen Cassiday and, as far as Marnell was concerned, the encounter could have waited yet another decade.

"Judge!" Cassiday called out, seemingly delighted.

"Hello Cassiday."

"Walking for exercise?" Cassiday asked.

"True." Marnell had suffered a slight heart attack his cardiologist had politely called a warning. He was well over sixty and felt every year of it.

Cassiday, on the other hand, looked good to Marnell except he still had a remembered facial tic near his left eye and his lips and skin were not a healthy color. He was a tall, late fiftyish man. He wore his expensive clothes well. Once he'd been a distance track star, a man who'd not allow himself to be beaten.

Marnell remembered what Justice Eston, of the state appellate court, had once told him about Cassiday: "The facial tic is strongest when he's either plotting to cheat someone or in the midst of the act."

Cassiday guided Marnell out of heavy pedestrian traffic.

"How long are you down for?" Cassiday asked solicitously.

"I've a small villa on the bay side of Siesta Key. I now inhabit it most of the year."

"Ah hah," Cassiday said. "Even the Florida television weather frauds admit we could have another several weeks of cold weather. I'm now a fanatic walker. Doctor's orders. Occasionally I cruise the malls looking for old acquaintances. How'd you like to walk in a great, uncrowded place, a place you'll want to walk even when the weather gets warm again?"

Marnell suddenly had a moment of recall concerning the court documents his office people had caught Cassiday changing.

"How much will it cost me?" he asked cautiously.

Cassiday smiled. "Not a Chinese quarter, Judge. The only payment is that you'll have to endure an occasional sales pitch from yours truly. I now make my living doing financial advice. You'll likely see a few old friends and enemies from Indianapolis." He removed a thick card from a fancy billfold and scribbled an address on the back. "Come tomorrow around eightish in the morning."

Marnell nodded, shook hands, and pocketed the card. His intention was to discard it as soon as possible. He walked a few minutes more in the mob and then fought the icy wind while he looked for his car in the mall's crowded parking area.

Cold.

Later, as he drank black coffee and ate a medically forbidden stale Danish inside his one-bath, one-bedroom villa, he dug the card out. The front was engraved, "Joe Cassiday, Advice," no address, no phone number. The address scribbled on the reverse was near US 41.

Marnell read the card again, remembering.

Cassiday had surely been the most corrupt lawyer who'd ever practiced in the Marion County Indianapolis courts. Cassiday's word was as valueless as a presidential candidate's and he'd robbed both rich and poor. He'd been an Olympic gold medal winner as a young man and he looked like an All American and so he'd lasted in practice almost twenty years, which showed something about the legal system.

Marnell hadn't seen the man since he'd testified against him at Cassiday's disbarment proceedings.

Marnell was now retired from the bench, retired from almost all except his own curiosity. He lived frugally and spent most of his time in libraries reading books on the Civil War, a ruthless era which fascinated him almost as much as his own, dangerous times. Kate, his wife, was now eleven years dead. There'd been no children.

He thought that if he visited the address Cassiday had provided it was likely Cassiday would seek some sort of revenge/repayment for the damning forgery testimony Marnell had provided the disciplinary committee.

There was another thing to remember: Vain, beautiful Kate had died because Cassiday, ten years younger than she, had pursued her, caught her, and then ignored her, breaking her heart. She'd died alone, driving her Buick into a tree at seventy plus miles an hour, leaving behind a confession note under his pillow that only Marnell had ever read. Marnell wondered if Cassiday was aware that he knew about the affair. He doubted it.

He sighed. Seeking vengeance was somewhat counter to his beliefs. And Kate was a long time dead.

Still . . .

At eight a.m. the next morning Marnell parked his Sable next to Lincolns, Cadillacs, and expensive foreign sports cars. The address found was that of a now abandoned school done in by a recent hurricane. The school was gone, but the windowless gymnasium next to it still looked to be in fair shape.

He shivered in the morning air and entered the gym.

There were already walkers, both male and female, a dozen or so in number. All wore bright-colored sweat suits and sported walking shoes. They walked under overhead lights around the edges of an old basketball court. In the center of the court there were folding chairs set up around a long table.

Cassiday waved to him. Cassiday was walking at near-running speed, a gazelle among elephants, always the show off. As he passed a sideline table the man flipped a bright penny onto a plate there while walking at high speed. He was half again as fast as any other walker, his facial tic almost absent during exercise.

Marnell took off his windbreaker and put it on a sideline table and began to walk at his regular speed. A late fiftyish woman fell in beside him at the second turn.

"First dayer," she said. "My name is Rose. The others will be most curious about you. Where and when did you know our fearless leader?"

"Indianapolis, I was once a judge there."

"Indianapolis was where he was suspended from practicing law wasn't it?" the woman asked.

Marnell nodded, wondering how she knew.

She laughed a little. "He tells us about such things when he spouts his early life heroics in his sales talks. He describes how bad people were to him up north during his early life."

"The disciplinary people were dead against him," Marnell answered stolidly. "He wasn't only suspended, he was disbarred for life."

"Fine." She picked up her pace. "Talk more to me at coffee time."

"Wait," he said, catching up to her. "What's the deal on his money plate? Are we supposed to contribute money to Joel Cassiday in some way? I'd not want any part of that."

"Wait and watch," she said and moved out faster than he cared to follow.

About nine o'clock Marnell saw Cassiday stop and examine the pennies on his plate. He then looked around to see how many walkers had become sitters. Almost all had. Cassiday cut across the basketball floor and pulled a wall chain that rang a bell.

All walking halted.

An old man in an apron and wearing thick glasses arthritically wheeled out a cart on which there were two coffee urns, regular and decaffeinated, plus a large silver pot of hot water for tea drinkers. The large cart also bore plates full of Danish pastries, doughnuts, toast, and a huge platter of scrambled eggs.

The walkers crowded around, filled plates, and sat at the long table.

Marnell got only a cup of black decaf, not wanting to obligate himself. He found a seat next to Rose. She was digging into a pile of scrambled eggs while she sipped tea.

"The eggs are cholesterol free," she said.

"Are you sure? Did you witness them being cooked?" he asked, never trusting Cassiday. "Tell me about the pennies."

She smiled, changing her face from plain to pretty.

"Twenty times around the floor perimeter is a mile. Cassiday's been medically ordered to do three to four miles a day for serious heart and circulatory problems. No more, no less. So he drops a penny on the plate each time around. When he estimates there are sixty to eighty he stops to check.

He has a poor memory for other than chicanery and so he uses the pennies to keep track."

"He carries pennies?"

"No. Look over there."

Marnell looked and saw a huge platter full of pennies on a corner table on the darker side of the gym. Somehow he'd missed seeing them during his own walking.

"I see."

He gazed around some more, recognizing some of the walkers.

He saw Jim Blanco, who'd once been C.E.O. of a failed savings and loan with downtown offices near the Circle plus two dozen branches around Indianapolis. He'd played bad golf with Blanco. He nodded at Blanco and Blanco grinned at him, perhaps remembering golfing victories. Marnell recalled that Cassiday, in his prime, had been general counsel for the S. and L. before it had been closed down by the federals and Blanco alone had been indicted.

In another chair Marnell spied George Prince. His contracting firm had built many downtown Indianapolis office buildings, then gone through receivership with Cassiday as the attorney, after the firm's money had inexplicably vanished.

Prince was inspecting him intently and so Marnell nodded. He drew a curt nod in return and remembered that Prince had little use for the world in general and lawyers/judges in particular.

Another man and several of the women looked familiar, but Marnell couldn't call them by name or place them in the old Indianapolis hierarchy in which he'd once held a part.

He tapped Rose on the shoulder. "How do you know Cassiday?"

"He picked me up on the beach one day." She smiled,

remembering. "I was willing. He's very pretty and I hereby admit my morals have never been what they ought to be." She held out a hand bearing three gaudy rings. "I think he saw these. They're real." She shook her head, remembering. "Then he discovered my car. I drive a Bentley convertible. After that he quickly cost me several hundred thousand dollars."

Marnell nodded, encouraging her to go on.

"For those dollars and a few nights of romance this New York City gal gets to walk free and wait for the golden boy to strike again. So far I've resisted his new schemes." She smiled again, this time painfully. "I have a lot of money left. Sooner or later, when all else fails, he'll concentrate on me and I'll get had and bedded once more."

"I see people here I think would most enjoy visiting Cassiday in a funeral home," Marnell said.

"Including me. Love and passion now turned to hidden hate. I admit it. I think all of us walkers hate him. How about you? All of us walkers are interested."

"I'm not the type who hates, but he stole money from me and then my wife."

"The rest of us hate. The pennies drive us wild," she said. "We keep conjecturing that if we could do something subtle about the pennies maybe he'd have a heart attack and we could all stand by idly and watch him die while we're getting ready to call emergency." She shook her head. "But he watches us closely and Rasputin, his old cook-bottlewasher-guard also watches."

"Rasputin? Is he the one who wheeled in the food cart?"

She nodded. "That's not his real name, but it's what we call him. He stands across the room from the penny plate and watches us walkers while he's preparing our breakfast."

"I wouldn't think he'd see much at his obvious age and

with those thick glasses," Marnell said.

Rose shrugged. "Maybe not. We're suspicious. Most of us get our day-to-day fun from turning down Cassiday's new schemes, frustrating him, then eating his free food and walking in his gymnasium at no cost."

Marnell thought for a moment. "I'm an observant man. Tomorrow I might find out for you and your walking friends if Rasputin sees what goes on around him. Just for fun, of course."

"Do that," she said encouragingly. "Do you play bridge?"

"Yes."

"Sometime we will play," she said, sounding what seemed a double meaning.

Later Marnell saw her talking intently to others.

The session concluded with Cassiday showing a video about the values of investing in precious metal coins, then generously offering to buy and hold the coins for all assembled, as trustee.

No one seemed overly interested.

The next morning Marnell arrived a little earlier. As he did his turns he nodded and sometimes waved at Rasputin who stood by his steam table where the food was kept before being served. Rasputin never nodded or waved back, unfriendly or, more likely, unseeing.

After a while, with Cassiday ahead of him, Marnell stole a penny, then another, then three at one time. Rasputin never blinked and Cassiday didn't notice.

Before Cassiday could do his final round Marnell guiltily threw the purloined pennies back into the plate.

Other walkers appeared to smile at Marnell until he dropped the pennies back in. Then they frowned.

As breakfast was served he whispered to Rose of his discovery and saw her spread the word. Some walkers nodded carefully, others seemed more animated.

Marnell thought Rose contacted all walkers except Cassiday.

On this second day the lecture concerned both bearer bonds and the purchase of old U.S. currency, with Cassiday being the buyer and holder for those interested.

When the lecture was done Cassiday approached Marnell.

"How about you, Judge? Anything in today's economics lesson strike you as usable?" His tic was present.

Marnell smiled. "On the day I saw you in the mall you told me that walking here wouldn't cost me a Chinese quarter. That's about all I own." It wasn't a complete lie. His judge's retirement kept him alive, but not into Cadillacs and/or Lincolns. There was a bank account and a few stocks and bonds.

"Got to keep your money moving or inflation will eat you," Cassiday said, looking shrewd and businesslike. "You own a villa and can borrow money on it. Surely . . ." The tic grew stronger.

Marnell nodded. "I'll keep listening."

Rose waited. As they exited she took his arm. "The bearer bonds he'd sell you would have little or no value and might even be stolen. The currency is overgraded and overpriced. I own a wad from a long time back."

Marnell nodded.

"Bridge tonight?" she asked.

"With whom?"

"Blanco and his wife. My place."

"All right."

Rose lived in a huge penthouse condo on Longboat, perhaps a million plus dollars worth of winter quarters. You could see miles of gulf beach and water plus golfers playing out their golden years from her balcony and windows.

Rose served weak drinks made with cheap whiskey.

Marnell learned that Blanco had done two years and was still on parole and that Blanco's wife could not mention Cassiday's name without adding a curse word.

Rose was a decent bridge player. Now and then, when she picked at him for a supposed misplay, Marnell refrained politely from telling her he was a life master.

Sometimes, when he was dummy, he'd hear the three other players whispering as he reentered the room after some kitchen errand Rose had sent him to accomplish.

"We're plotting," Rose said. "Do you want to be a part of our plot? We'd like that. Time fleets and we grow older."

Marnell believed she was serious. He shook his head.

The bridge players nodded coldly.

"Bull crap to you," said Blanco's wife.

"I like you," Rose said at her door when bridge was done and the bad language Blancos had vanished into the warm night. "I could like you more. Want to stay the night?"

He nodded his head and gave her an awkward kiss. "Why not?"

He stayed the night. Most of what he got, other than minor bed games, were reasons to enlist in the anti-Cassiday cause.

The following morning she said fretfully. "He brings new people in now and then, just as he brought you. Maybe he'll bring someone else soon. Someone stronger than you."

"I don't like him, but I'm not a killer," Marnell said stolidly.

On the mornings that followed he decided not to whisper about other faults he found in Cassiday's alarm system. For example he found he could put added pennies in Cassiday's plate one day, then take pennies out the next so that the exercise might be irregular. Always, before Cassiday was finished with his walk, Marnell corrected his plate count.

After the morning walks Cassiday tried, day after day, to sell, first junk bonds, then commodities, and later Mexican and Chinese stock market items. Four mornings in a row he tried to market a foolproof system for determining what companies were about to be bought out by larger companies.

No one seemed to be buying his plans. Cassiday continued bravely.

To encourage himself to join the conspirators Marnell had taken to reading Kate's last letter each night. He found himself growing more angry at Cassiday.

On a bright mid-February day a new man came to the gymnasium, brought by Rose. The newcomer was thin, old, and brown from the sun and weather. Rose introduced him to Cassiday and the man then fell in beside Cassiday and kept pace with him for a time, then passed him, moving even faster than Cassiday.

Cassiday quickened his pace. The air became full of race electricity.

After completing his own next lap Marnell stopped and watched the race. The new walker walked like a distance man and Cassiday doggedly pursued, an Olympian waiting for the proper time to win.

On and on. Pennies rattled in Cassiday's plate.

The walking ended suddenly when Cassiday made one great leap high into the air that passed the interloper, then fell to the floor. He lay gasping for air.

Rasputin walked to the bell and rang it, stopping all.

"Someone call emergency," Rose instructed.

No one moved.

Marnell went to the fallen man. Cassiday seemed not to be

breathing. The tic was gone. Cassiday's color was blue, but he smiled as if he'd accomplished something great.

"Does anyone know CPR?" Marnell called.

No one responded.

"Emergency ambulance on the way," Blanco said. "I just called."

When the ambulance had departed with Cassiday's lifeless body the runners lingered. Rasputin, true to his job to the last, served up cholesterol-free eggs, rolls, toast, coffee, and tea.

The runner who'd walked Cassiday into the ground had vanished.

Marnell stood and pointed accusingly around the table.

"Some or all of you killed him," he accused. "Not that it matters, but I believe you'll get away with it." He looked down at Rose. "Where'd you get your new friend?"

"Boston," she said. "Second in his age group in the east, heel and toe seniors. Executive V.P. of a bank where I do much business."

"Did you pay him to come?"

"Of course not. He's an old friend who winters south of here in Venice." She smiled carefully. "How was I to know Cassiday would try to out-walk him? Surely you don't believe that I . . ."

Marnell looked around. "Someone from the police will come to investigate." He looked at the cart full of goodies and the old chef, Rasputin. "Did you call the police?"

"Not me," Rasputin said. "He was three months back on my pay. And he got my nest egg a year back on junk bonds. I think he was almost broke. I ain't calling no damned police. Old people die from too much exercise every day in Florida."

Marnell shook his head. "If the police come my own opinion will be that Cassiday committed his own kind of suicide. None of you would allow yourselves to be cheated again by him and so he had nothing much to live for. Besides, he was a fool. He owns a walking track and then invites, feeds, and provides exercise for enemies. Deliberate suicide, but perhaps not."

Several walkers looked worried at his last statement.

"I'm going to walk over to the wall and turn out all the lights. While it's dark you might dispose of anything you have in your possession that could be a problem should the police arrive and decide we should all be searched."

He walked to the wall and pulled the circuit breaker switch down. The big gymnasium, without many outside windows, went dark.

He heard the tiny clinking of coins, then nothing. He waited a suitable time, then pulled the switch back on.

The table bore a heap of pennies, several dozen of them.

Blanco watched Marnell with distrust. "You're now going to make sure the police do come here, aren't you, Marnell? You always were a righteous bastard. You've made yourself up some kind of crappy story to tell about Cassiday committing suicide. But if that doesn't wash all the rest of us will get stepped on when you testify for the prosecution after they find our fingerprints on those pennies. They'll then figure we all killed the golden boy."

George Prince nodded. "If we weren't the civilized ninnies we are I'd ask everyone present to join together one more time and do you in for a morning desert, Judge Marnell."

"Maybe," Blanco began. "I'm still on parole. Maybe we ought . . ."

Rasputin nodded. So, finally, did Rose.

Marnell felt a touch of alarm. "All of you misjudge me. As I said Cassiday either committed suicide or died as the result of a tragic accident."

He sighed then, not liking the idea of personal confession.

"Trust me," he said softly.

He dug deep in his pockets and threw his own two cents worth (times four) into the pot. He'd not had time on this morning to return the pennies to the plate even if he'd wanted to. Now Cassiday was dead and by showing the pennies to the others it was far too late to make a return. Besides, keeping them had felt extra good this morning.

"All for one," he said.

There were smiles.

"Does anyone know what the financial arrangement is on this gymnasium?" he asked. "This is a great place to walk."

Blanco nodded. "I know about it. Cassiday rented it from a bank by the month. I know the people at the bank. Should we try to assume the rental?"

Marnell gave them his most judicious nod.

"Of course we should," he said. "A gymnasium in Cassiday's Olympic memory." He turned from Blanco to Rasputin.

"Wash every penny sunshine clean," he instructed.

Argent Blood

April 13: Today I made a discovery. I was allowed to look in the mirror in Doctor Mesh's office. I'm about forty years old, judging from my face and hair. I failed to recognize me, and by this I mean there is apparently no correlation between what I saw of me in the mirror and this trick memory of mine. But it's good to see one's face, although my own appears ordinary enough.

I must admit to more interest in the pretty bottles on Doctor Mesh's shelves than my face. Somewhere in dreams I remember bottles like those. I wanted the bottles so badly that a whirling came in my head. But I didn't try to take them, as I suspected that Doctor Mesh was watching closely.

Doctor Mesh said, "You're improving. Soon we'll give you the run of our little hospital and grounds, except, of course, the disturbed room." He pinched me on the arm playfully. "Have to keep you healthy."

I nodded and was delighted and the sickness inside went away. Then I could take my eyes off the shelves of bottles— nice ones full of good poisons—some that I recognized vaguely, others that struck no chord.

There would be another time.

Later I went back into the small ward—my home—the only one I really remember. Miss Utz smiled at me from her desk and I lay on my bed and watched her. She has strange, bottomless eyes. When I see her, the longing to be normal again is strongest. But the disturbances recur.

My ward is done in calm colors. The whole effect is soporific. I'm sure I never slept so much or dreamed so much. Bottles, bottles.

The food is good and I eat a great deal. My weight seems to remain fairly constant, decreasing when I'm disturbed, coming back to normal when released.

My fellow patients are not so well off. Most of them are very old and either idiotic or comatose. Only the man with the beard is rational enough to talk to sometimes.

The bearded man saw me watching him. "Pet!" he yelled at me. He makes me very angry sometimes. He's always saying that to me when he's disturbed. I wonder what he means?

I shall quit writing for the day. Doctor Mesh says it's good to keep a diary, but I'm afraid someone will read this. That would anger me, and extreme anger brings on disturbances.

I'm sleepy now.

April 18: I've got to stop this sort of thing. I tried again with the bearded man, but he won't drink water that he hasn't freshly drawn. I think he suspected that I'd done something, because he watched me malevolently for a long time.

I came out of the disturbed room yesterday, sick and weak, remembering nothing of that time.

No one seems to have found the bottle I hid the day I became disturbed, a bottle empty now down to the skull and crossbones, but to no purpose except the bearded man's anger. I wonder why Doctor Mesh angers me so? And Miss Utz? I guess it must be because they move and talk and exist. The old ones who don't move and talk to me don't anger me —only the bearded man and Doctor Mesh and Miss Utz.

But nothing seems to work on the Doctor or Miss Utz and the bearded man is very careful.

Today, at mid-morning, Miss Utz helped me down to the

solarium and I sat there for a while. Outside, the flowers have begun to bloom and some minute purple and green creepers are folding their way over the walls around this tiny asylum. They look very good and poisonous.

My neck itched and I scratched at the places until they bled and Miss Utz laughed her cold laugh and put antiseptic on my neck. She told me that this is a private asylum run on private funds, taking no patients but hopeless ones that have been confined elsewhere for years before transfer here. If that is completely so, then why am I here?

In the afternoon Doctor Mesh tested my reflexes and listened to my heart. He says I'm in good physical condition. He seemed happy about that. He was evasive when I asked him if I'd ever be well, and that made me angry. I managed to hide all outward signs of my feeling.

When I was back in the ward and Miss Utz was temporarily out of sight, the feel of the poison bottle comforted me.

April 30: The dreams are growing worse. So clear and real. I dreamed I was in Doctor Mesh's office. I could see the pretty bottles on the shelves. Miss Utz and Doctor Mesh were reading my diary and laughing. The bearded man kept screaming at me from far away. The dream was very real, but my eyes would not open.

This morning the bearded man is watching me from his bed. He looks very weak, but he had a disturbance this week. Being disturbed is very hard on one, Doctor Mesh once told me.

I was in Doctor Mesh's office for a while earlier and got to look in the mirror. I did not recognize me again. Sometimes I feel as if my head had been cut open, the contents scrambled, and then recapped. There is no pain, but there is no place to search for things.

A little while ago I tried something from the new bottle that I'd taken from Doctor Mesh's office. It didn't work. Nothing works—even though I saw Miss Utz drink some of the water.

May 2: I shall have to hide this diary. I'm almost sure they are reading it. They brought the bearded man back from "disturbed" today. His eyes are red and sunken and he kept watching me all morning. When Miss Utz left the ward he beckoned me over with an insistent finger.

He said nothing. Instead he lifted his beard away and pointed at his throat. I looked at it, but could see nothing but some small, red marks, as if he'd cut himself with his fingernails. He pulled one of the cuts open with hands that shook and a tiny driblet of blood pulsed out. He laughed.

I looked away, the blood making me feel ill.

The corner of one of the pages in this diary is torn. I didn't tear it.

May 3: I talked to the bearded man today—if talk can describe the conversation we had. He's insistent. He said I can't know when they feed on me as I'm in a sort of seizure and that I'm their "pet" because I'm young and strong. He made me check my neck and there are red marks on it. He said they let me steal the poisons because they know I can't harm them.

He told me I killed three people outside, poisoned them. He says I was a pharmacist outside, but now I'm incurably insane and can't ever be released. He said I was in a state hospital for years before I came here. I don't remember it.

He claims that Doctor Mesh and Miss Utz are vampires.

I went back to my bed when he let me get away and spent a fairly restful afternoon. I dreamed of bottles on the shelf and something came to me in the dream—a thing all perfect like myself.

The bearded man says that we could kill them with silver bullets, but the thought of a gun is abhorrent to me.

I've never really believed in that sort of thing, but what if the bearded man is right? What if Doctor Mesh and Miss Utz are vampires? This place would be perfect for them. No investigation of death, no legal troubles, patients forgotten years ago. Take only the incurables, the forgotten. A regular supply.

But the plan, so intricate and perfect. I will have to have the bearded man's help. He will have to steal the things I want. If they are watching me, laughing when I steal from them, it would be too risky for me to take it.

May 4: We began the plan today. The bearded man managed to steal the large bottle of saline solution and the tube and needle to introduce it into the veins. He also managed the other part. The chemical was where I'd described it as being on Doctor Mesh's shelves. I even had the color of the bottle right. Now we must wait for the right time. Perhaps tonight?

I shall hide this book well.

May 6: I am in fever. We did not manage until last night, and it took a very long time. I feel all steamy inside and there is a dizziness.

I'm trying for anger and a disturbance. Miss Utz is watching from her desk, her eyes hot and bright.

They will take me to the disturbed room.

May 9: A few lines. I'm ill. Nothing seems to be working inside me and the heat is such that my eyes see more brightness than shade. I'm in the disturbed room and I've seen no one alive all day. I can hear the bearded man's whiny laugh, and once I heard him clap his hands.

I think they are dead. They must be dead.

We put the silver chloride in the saline solution and put the needle in my arm and let it all flow inside. When I was disturbed they must have fed on me.

If I rise up I can see the toe of a female foot right at the door and it's all curled and motionless. I can't see Doctor Mesh, but he must be there in the hall near Miss Utz.

Dead of my poisoned blood, my fine and intricate blood. A new specific for vampires. *Silver Blood.*

I wish this heat would go away. Three outside and two in here. I want there to be time for more . . .

Whistler

"I'd like you to go with me to Hill Hospital today," Senator Adams said. He nodded me toward the old leather couch in his office. He then made an alleyway between the law books stacked on his desk so he could see me. I sat. He was obviously researching something and I was pretty sure I knew what it was. The stacks of books piled on his desk, in corners, and here and there on the floor were even larger than usual.

"What are you researching?" I asked, to confirm my suspicions.

"Insanity," he said. "It seems to be a poor defense. We let lay jurors determine sanity in the same trial they're also primarily asked to determine guilt or innocence."

"You don't agree with our laws on sanity?" I asked, unshocked.

He gave me a somewhat sour look. "Read the case reports, Robak. They'll show you that few people using the defense do well if the crime charged was violent."

"Hill Hospital and Sam Whitley are what you're thinking on then?"

He nodded.

Hill was a mental hospital.

"What time do you go?"

"About three this afternoon. I'd like you with me when I talk with Dr. Ansberg and perhaps see Sam Whitley."

"I've an appointment for then," I said. "And Sam Whitley's your client, not mine."

"Please change your appointment." He gave me an apologetic look. "For me it's doctor's orders. You inherit the case."

"Thank you," I said. Some small sarcasm may have shown through for he gave me a sharp look. I kept my own face impassive by busying myself looking around his cluttered office. Sam Whitley had been indicted on two counts of murder and, from what I'd read in the local paper, the prosecutor had no proof problems. Area media had viciously reported all the bloody facts of the murders.

I was three years into the practice of law at that time. I was still sure of many things. I got better at being unsure as I grew older and watched the world undo itself around me.

"Sam cut my yard when he was a boy," the senator said in explanation.

He was no longer a state senator, but the name had stuck. Once a state senator always a state senator.

"I heard your yard cutter exploded again at the jail and it got to be a toss-up whether Judge Steinmetz would send him to the reformatory to await trial or on to Hill Hospital for observation," I said.

"He did go berserk again. He isn't large, but it took three deputies to overpower him. Judge Steinmetz held a hearing and sensibly decided he needed to be examined at Hill." He smiled and looked out his grimy window at the city of Bington below, now in full-leaf summer. The city was his love now that his wife was gone. He was a good man, but sometimes his ideas on the law and how it should operate were odd. He gave me a penetrating look. "Tell me your opinion on the current state of the insanity defense."

"In Sam Whitley's case?"

"Yes."

"It won't mean a thing. The prosecutor will undoubtedly present a dozen witnesses to testify Whitley was sane and normal around the time of the murders. Even if we get favorable opinions from psychiatrists it's up to a jury to make the final decision and you know few violent murderers get off. Of course if psychiatrists testify and then Judge Steinmetz rules Whitley not sane enough to assist us or stand trial then we'd be off the hook until that changed."

He nodded again.

"What made you take the case?" I asked bluntly. "I mean here's a man who, in a fit of rage, lays in wait and kills his estranged wife and her lover with an ax. The newspapers keep calling him Sam Borden. I suppose that's after Lizzie Borden of forty-whacks fame. It isn't your kind of case."

"I remembered him as a boy. Also Judge Steinmetz appointed me—us—to defend him." He shook his head sadly. "When Sam cut my yard and Steinmetz's yard down the street he whistled and smiled all the time he was working. A happy boy then. A whistler."

"So we go to Hill Hospital this afternoon to see if the psychiatrists will say your whistler's sane enough for trial?"

"Yes. I called Dr. Ansberg last night. He's an old friend. He told me Sam's coming along slowly. I'd like you to read the file and be ready to go with me today."

I took the file and hefted it. "Thin," I said. "Very light."

"There's a few things you won't find in there. The new boy friend had moved in with Sam's wife. He was a volunteer part-time deputy sheriff. He ran Sam off with a gun twice when Sam went there attempting a reconciliation. Sam lost one family to a fire and a cheating wife to a man with a gun." He looked at me and shook his head. "She laughed at Sam."

I called and changed my appointment. It didn't make me like Sam Whitley's case any better. It was a dead sure loser.

The file contained both Whitley's juvenile record and his adult record, a copy of an old pre-sentence report, plus a sheaf of news stories about the murders and Sam's arrest. There were also two scathing editorials clipped from the pages of the local paper. That paper has, down the years, found it profitable to be against major and minor sins.

Whitley had come whistling out of what seemed to be a normal boyhood. He'd been in no trouble until after he was fifteen. His intelligence was slightly below normal, but not low enough to take him out of regular school. In his fifteenth year he'd been orphaned in a home fire in which his parents, older sister, and younger brother had died. He'd been the sole scorched survivor. A Christmas tree fire, lights left on after the family had gone to bed.

Maybe we could lean on that, stir up sympathy. It might keep him off death row.

Maybe.

His problems had begun after the fire. There'd been social security and so he'd been a wanted commodity. Custody had originally passed to an aged uncle who'd used the money Sam had brought for his alcohol habit. That arrangement hadn't lasted. There'd been a string of foster homes. There'd soon been drugs and break-ins, stolen cars, and fights. He'd robbed a grocery store with a cap pistol and drawn a term at Youth School. He'd critically knifed another inmate there, a bigger, older boy who'd threatened him sexually. Then, when Sam had turned eighteen and become eligible for adult prison, he'd soon made it.

I looked over the record. From the bare bones I could see nothing he'd done had ever been clever or planned well. *A dumbhead.*

On parole he'd married and for a time had stayed out of trouble. She'd cheated and he'd caught her, beaten her savagely, and so gone back to prison. She'd filed for divorce. When his sentence was up Sam had followed her to her family home out Moss Road near the river. Police theorized in news articles that if her mother had been home she might also have died by the avenging ax. Sam had hewed wife and boy friend to bits, then charged the police who'd come at a neighbor's call, still swinging the bloody ax. What was left of Sam's wife and her lover had been found scattered about the house.

I thought about the pictures that would be introduced at trial and shook my head.

No chance for the whistling boy. Life or death.

Dr. Ansberg was a tall, old man with a fringe of dyed black hair around an otherwise bald head. He had a hard-to-believe Viennese accent and his face consisted mostly of bright dentures. He clasped the senator's hand warmly and I could see they liked each other. He nodded formally at me when we were introduced.

"Your partner and I have known each other for many years. When I first came to this country I met him at church. He helped me greatly, Mr. Robak."

"You helped me also, Doctor," the senator said. "You talked me back to work when my wife died. You went out of your way." He smiled at Ansberg and at me. I'd found he had a thousand friends and that he deserved them. Sometimes I didn't understand him, but I loved the old man.

"The senator saved me," Ansberg continued.

"How's that?" I asked, interested.

"When I came here they were going to fire me from this place. That was when my English wasn't so good. I was already growing old and my wife was ill. There were many reasons I needed my job here." He smiled and the dentures sparkled. "The senator made one phone call and my job was saved. He charged me nothing. He wouldn't even send me a bill."

The senator looked embarrassed. "Enough. Tell us about our man Whitley."

"He grows better," Dr. Ansberg said, smiling tranquilly. "Perhaps soon we'll have him able to assist you in his trial."

"But you and those helping you couldn't testify he's sane and competent now?"

"I believe not yet. When they assigned him to me he was still quite violent. Paranoid schizophrenia. We tranquilized him. There are truly remarkable drugs available for many purposes these days. He fell into a pattern which I could predict. He first forgot what had happened. The drugs allowed him to withdraw from life for a time. He's now turned back a bit toward us and life. He remembers his childhood, his early youth, his happy times. He has no memory yet of the fire which took his family, his prison days, or the killings. Those things are below the surface. They'll be the last to return. I believe he has vague dreams of them, flashes, insights into himself. With the drugs all seems well most of the time." He nodded. "We push him along the stream. My prognosis is he'll soon be well enough to stand trial." He looked out the window of his office and got up. "Come see him yourselves."

I followed the senator to the window. Outside white-clad attendants and patients moved slowly or briskly, as they desired, under the warm summer sun. Some patients gazed vacantly, others seemed occupied with themselves.

"Sun time," Dr. Ansberg said. "This time of year we try to get even those who've lost all contact with us out into the summer world."

I recognized Sam Whitley from newspaper pictures. He was accompanied by two attendants, both of them burly men. Sam came smiling down the walk, his stride boyish. He was, I knew, in his early thirties.

The senator shook his head sadly. "Too bad for him he

can't remain the way he now is and come no further."

Dr. Ansberg regarded the senator solemnly. "Yes? Too bad?"

"Soon he'll be trying to swim in rough seas, trying to live or die," the senator said. "The prosecutor talked to me earlier today." He looked over at me and frowned. "He's going for the death penalty." He looked away from me and back down at Sam Whitley, who walked lightly and uncaringly on.

"That's unfair," I said. "It was a family thing. Certainly his wife had given him provocation. There's the unwritten law." I thought quickly about the trial to come, about bloody clothes, gory color pictures, and a semi-competent prosecutor running for his political life in an election year. "It's unfair," I said again.

"Life's unfair," the senator said evenly. He nodded at the happy boy-man below. "Unfair, but legal."

Dr. Ansberg watched only Senator Adams. His eyes were serious as he watched; his smile had vanished.

Ansberg and another doctor from Hill Hospital appeared in court ten days later and testified Sam Whitley was still unable to assist his attorneys in his defense. Judge Steinmetz continued the matter.

Prosecutor Paul Roberts, sensing trial delay past election time, held an angry press conference, then filed a new petition asking that other psychiatrists be appointed to examine Sam Whitley. Steinmetz denied it without a hearing. The prosecutor made vague statements about an appeal, but none was filed. He did use what had happened in his campaign speeches. Judges are easy for the public to hate even when they're right.

Summer dragged into fall. In November Roberts narrowly lost his bid for another term as prosecutor. Senator Adams and I bought each other a celebration drink.

After the election a rapist-murderer terrified the local university campus. He killed three young women in Jack the Ripper style. The news media forgot Sam Whitley and took up a new cause. Then a many times convicted drunk driver, operating without a license, drove a plush stolen auto unerringly into six schoolchildren waiting for a school bus. All of the children were under ten. The driver killed two, maimed two more. Angry protesters paraded in front of the jail and courthouse.

Sam Whitley grew cooler.

The new prosecutor came and conferred calmly with Senator Adams and me about Whitley and his circumstances.

"They say he's still about as he was," he said. "I went up there to Hill and his doctor, a nice old man named Ansberg, was very cooperative. He let me see him in his ward. I wasn't allowed to ask questions. Ansberg explained that Whitley's hold on reality is quite fragile."

Senator Adams nodded. "If you'd have asked one of us would have gone along. Within the limits of what Dr. Ansberg would have allowed we'd have let you ask him whatever you wanted."

Alvin Koontz, the new prosecutor, said, "I really don't need anything from him. We've a God's plenty of evidence sitting in the police lock room gathering dust. All I need is for the hospital people to say he's competent to stand trial."

"We're ready when Whitley's ready," the senator said. "You were the one most recently at Hill. What did Ansberg tell you?"

Koontz smiled. He was a good man and an excellent lawyer. The senator and I both approved of him.

"He said Sam Whitley was still hiding back in his boyhood. Dr. Ansberg took me past the locked ward where they

73

keep him. He was whistling and bouncing a ball off a wall and trying to catch it." He shook his head. "He had a big smile. He seemed happy. Yes, happy." He looked out the senator's window at the snow falling on Bington's dirty downtown. "It was a better day than today. I tried to talk with the other doctor, but he didn't have much to say. Ansberg appears to be very much the one in charge. He seemed to think Sam Whitley might stay as he is for a long time, still living a fantasy life around the age of fourteen or so, unmarred by all that happened afterward." Koontz seemed uneasy about it. "Is that possible, Senator?"

"I suppose. What are your intentions, Alvin?"

"I'll prosecute him if he recovers, gentlemen. I looked over the file. I don't know for certain that I'd ask for the death penalty."

"You're generous in thinking of that."

Koontz shook his head. "Not generous. It's only that time has passed. And Ansberg seems to think that Sam Whitley may stay in limbo. He could go either way tomorrow or stay as he is. If he doesn't recover I suppose we'll never prosecute him. You gentlemen know the law doesn't allow that." He smiled once more. "The thing that really got to me in seeing him was that he seemed happy."

"He's had much unhappiness. You know his history?"

"I've looked at his file, Senator. I know about the fire and his dead wife's reputation."

"Perhaps he's already had his punishment," the senator said, his eyes strange. He seemed nervous, slightly upset. "Maybe it works that way. Some of us get our punishment up front and commit our crimes afterward."

"The Campus Creeper didn't. We start trial on him next month. He's nineteen and comes from a good family, Senator." He shook his head in disbelief. "Nineteen . . ." He thought for a moment. "Then there's that multiple-vehicle homicide case to try. No rest for an already weary new prosecutor."

Perhaps things would have stayed *in status quo* longer, but Ansberg suffered a heart attack in May.

I heard about it when I arrived at the office on a bright morning. The senator was already there, moving about his office restlessly, shelving books, discarding papers, and obviously waiting for me.

"Dr. Ansberg's over in the Bington Hospital in intensive care. He's sent word he wants to see me. You can come if you say nothing—no matter what Ansberg says—while we're with him. I want you to come. Ansberg's wife is long dead, his only daughter was last heard of in a commune and can't be found and he had no sons."

"Why does he want to see you?"

He shrugged. He seemed calm.

"Did you know Ansberg had medical problems?"

"We're both of that age," he said, smiling now. "Terminal."

I tagged along because he wanted me. I drove him to the hospital.

Intensive care was on the fifth floor. A stout nurse led us down a quiet hall and gave us stern instructions. She shook her head when the senator inquired concerning Ansberg's condition.

Ansberg lay quietly in a hospital bed. He seemed shrunken. He had tubes in one nostril. A suspended bottle dripped clear fluid into another tube needled into his arm. He had wires attached to his arms and chest. Someone had removed the too-white dentures.

The room smelled of antiseptic and ammonia.

Ansberg's eyes were still alert but wounded. They followed Senator Adams across the hospital room.

"Sit," Ansberg ordered him in a hoarse whisper, ignoring me.

The senator pulled up a metal folding chair. I found an inconspicuous place near the window of the small room.

Ansberg began without preamble. Each word seemed an effort. "I think your man Sam Whitley will now be all right."

"You mean he'll be competent to stand trial?" the senator asked.

"No, not that. I believe he'll remain always as he is now." He grimaced an imitation smile. "There are other disciplines than yours of law, Senator," he said carefully. "Surely you realize that?"

The senator shrugged.

Ansberg continued, "Sometimes, when I began to treat him, he seemed to be coming along despite what I did. I gave him shock treatments for a time until that stopped. I gave him other drugs than the tranquilizers. I spent hours—no, days—going over his early life with him, again and again. Progress stagnated. He believes now that he's contagiously ill and fancies someday he'll be well enough to be reunited with his family. His mind is no longer inquiring or curious. He wanted to forget. I helped him forget. He believes he's fourteen. Time has stopped for him, fourteen forever." Ansberg shook his head. "I've not had to do anything with him for a long while. Only the normal tranquilizers now."

Senator Adams leaned close to Ansberg, but I saw that the senator's eyes were on me. "I didn't ask you to do this, Doctor."

Ansberg's voice weakened. "I know. Perhaps I saw it wrong, read it poorly. What I've done might even be criminal. I know little of your laws. But there are more types of insanity than my profession yet has names for. If Sam Whitley recovers he must then stand trial, perhaps even die. You saw in Sam the boy who once was happy and made me see that boy also. Now he'll always be that boy. As once you gave me a free gift which meant my life I've now given a life gift to Sam Whitley in your name. I'll let your legal mind fumble about and decide whether what I've done is tolerable or not, whether it's 'right.' It may not be to you. Perhaps what I sensed in watching you was wrong. But believe *it is* the way I've revealed and can't be easily changed. You may, if you wish, ask that new psychiatrists be assigned for Sam Whitley at Hill. You may then tell them what I've done and what I'm telling you now. They'll find nothing in the medical charts to help them because I put very little there. Perhaps, but only perhaps, they'll manage to turn your Sam Whitley forward again if that's what you desire." He gave us the smile-grimace again. "If you do nothing then perhaps things will proceed at their normal, legal snail's pace. Sam Whitley will remain as he is and be soon forgotten. He'll stay always as he is now. Your choice, Senator." Once more he smiled his ghastly, joking smile, sans teeth.

The senator shook his head and looked inquiringly over at me. I realized, at that moment, that he'd at least suspected and probably known what was going on. Several times, in the past months, he'd visited Hill Hospital alone.

"That would let a guilty man escape punishment," he said.

"Yes," Ansberg admitted. "And something more. It might also let an insane man regain sanity, limited sanity, but a sanity which brought him happiness."

In the car I looked the senator over. "You're a most devious man. I'm sure you knew what Ansberg was doing."

He shook his head wearily. "I never knew for certain. Perhaps I suspected." He faced me. "Don't start the motor yet. We need to make a decision."

"We need to get to Judge Steinmetz and tell him exactly what's happened," I said harshly.

"Think some on it. If Sam Whitley had been convicted what would have happened to him?"

"Perhaps the death penalty. Some get it."

"Come off it, Robak. You're a better lawyer than that. Koontz would have never tried to get it. Even if he had, at trial level or appellate level, after ten thousand hours of agonizing briefs and arguments, the death penalty would have vanished in smoke and we'd have won a great victory. What then would have happened to Sam Whitley?"

"A long time in prison."

"Yes, but eventually parole?"

"Maybe," I admitted grudgingly. "Usually."

"Almost assuredly if Sam lived long enough. Do you think that prison time would have turned Sam into a solid citizen?"

"I don't know." I thought about it and finally shook my head. "I suppose not."

"You know not. Isn't what's happening to him now, under Ansberg's cure, an effective method of containing Whitley?"

"It isn't a legal method."

"Quit being scandalized because the lawbooks don't specify it. You know they aren't the answer to all."

"People get out of mental hospitals also," I warned.

"No. Civilly committed people get out. Whitley can't get out. If he should move forward and become able, in the future, to assist in his defense then he goes back to jail and from there to trial. The evidence in this one will last until the last survivor witness dies. Think about it, Robak."

I thought. I thought for a long time.

Ansberg died four days later. Senator Adams died in 1974.

A few days ago I had the necessity, as judge, to go to Hill Hospital. There, after holding hearings, I paid a courtesy call on the new superintendent. He seemed harried and complained of being overworked and understaffed. I didn't mention Sam Whitley's name.

When I left his office I drove to the north gate, taking the route past the locked ward where Sam Whitley had once been held.

He was, I knew, no longer there.

Near the north gate, in front of a pleasant building surrounded by shrubs and flowers, I saw Sam Whitley. There were no longer guards watching him. I slowed and he gave my car a glance. He was now bent with age, not as spry as once he'd been. There was a basketball goal and he had a ball. He was pretty good. I waved and he nodded back to me, smiling. He then went intently back to his game.

I was almost sure he was whistling.

Watcher

The cemetery now claimed to be the ritziest cemetery in the city. The new corporation erected a brick border wall with a wide entrance and had begun opening roads into new sections. A fine scroll sign above the entrance read "Rosemont Cemetery."

Chester "Chet" Jones had worked in the old cemetery for long years. Now he worked for Scallin.

Martin Scallin owned a small piece of the action and managed the graveyard. He liked to tell jokes about the cemetery like: "People are dying to get in here."

And, in truth, there are few places where a salesman sells land for as much per acre as in a cemetery.

Scallin was a man whose pants always needed hitching up. He'd managed his own life poorly and so he despised the world around him that hadn't rewarded him. The cemetery was potentially the best deal he'd ever had. He was determined it would be a success. *No matter what.*

Chet hated him.

Rosemont sprawled along a quiet hill in the western part of the southern city. West town was expensive. There were fine houses, ritzy business and professional buildings, and classy private schools. The corporation had bought out the old cemetery people after optioning all available land around it and so making it impossible for the graveyard to expand. The old group, outgunned and bankrupt, had capitulated. They'd sold.

Sales were slow, but Scallin was sure they'd pick up now

summer was almost over. The boiler room telephone bank was in operation and mass mailings had gone out from the post office. If those didn't work, then the corporation would try personable door to door sales people.

Where will you spend eternity?

Chet was the only holdover from the former operation and he was nervously awaiting his pink slip.

Chet could see Scallin surveying him on this day. Chet's shoes were muddy and he wore old corduroys and steel-rimmed glasses, but he did know the cemetery. When visitors came Chet could lead them to any grave.

Chet knew Scallin wanted to fire him, but needed him for now.

Soon.

"I get the report we opened a new grave in the 'N' section and the diggers said there was a crazy, black lady making noise with pots and pans," Scallin said.

Chet shrugged noncommittally. "That'd be Hattie Jones. Section N is near the edge of the original graveyard. She comes around and guards old graves some years."

Scallin shook his head. "We're trying to sell the last of the old lots so we can raise money to complete the roads without assessing the stockholders. Having a crazy lady hanging around ain't a help. You hike up there and talk sense to her. Her last name's the same as yours. You kin?"

Chet nodded. "Yes."

He nodded after he was outside. *They won't fire me today.*

Chet found Hattie Jones in the old section. She was ancient and fierce where he was peaceful. She had a dead half-brother buried in the old grounds, but it wasn't his grave alone she came to visit. And partly, Chet knew, she also came to see him.

Today she was wearing multiple layers of dirty clothes despite the heat. She had a battered three-wheel baby buggy full of canned food, cooking utensils, clothes, plus the things she used in her rituals. She was thin and her eyes were intent. A sticky fly kept buzzing her.

He nodded, never sure how she'd treat him.

"Good to see you my sweet Chet," she said, smiling. "It's been a long while since you run off from me at the project."

"Yes," he said.

"You know it's the year again. A year that can be divided by four. That's the time them two, the ones that shot Ned, want to rise back out with their hanging ropes and burning crosses."

Chet nodded. In adjoining graves there were buried two men who'd died in a wild shootout on the long ago night when Ned had also been killed. Elizabeth did ritual around their graves.

The old owners had deemed it harmless.

"New folks bought out this cemetery," he said. He pointed out and around. "A corporation. They have rules about visitation and closing hours. They need to sell the rest of the burial plots in the old graveyard area. They got people selling on telephones."

"They sell lots to black people?" she asked belligerently.

"Sure. Anyone who can pay. Things ain't black and white now."

She waited. The world was still green around them. Birds sang. The fly left Elizabeth and bothered him.

"They sent me to tell you they don't want you here," Chet said uncomfortably. "You can't do anything other than just visit."

"I ain't here that much," she answered reasonably. "I sleep most nights in the project just like you did before you run off from me."

"Sleeping's only part of it. They don't want you doing anything more than just coming in for like an hour or two maybe once a week."

"Are they white men?"

"No. Some are black. It's a corporation."

She visibly thought on it. "You go back and tell them I got to be around for a little while. Tell them I'll promise not to start no more cookin' fires. When harvest moon comes, real soon now, things will be quiet again. But I got to stay. Otherwise them dead men could bother Ned in his grave. Ned don't want or need that." She nodded at him. "I know you never believed what I tried teaching you so long ago, but it's true." She reached in her possessions and brought out a large crucifix with one missing arm. She pointed it toward two graves, side by side. "These was bad dudes, but Ned, he fixed them when they come. Now these two layin' there next to each other are still plottin'." She nodded. "What I do now for Ned I'd do for you."

Chet remembered the bloody shootout. Ned and the two white men dead, five other men wounded. It had been almost fifty years ago. Things had changed, but Chet wasn't sure they were better.

"The corporation might law you," he advised her.

She smiled. "They oughtn't to do that. You know I got friends at the newspaper. Wrote a nice story four years back. I'd call them if I got lawed. Tell your rich corporation people to let me be until harvest moon, sweetie. I got do do this."

Chet nodded. "I'll say what you said."

The corporation, wary of bad publicity after Chet's report to Scallin, put guards on the main gate, plus they hired on a special guard named Billy Bob to watch Elizabeth. When she absented herself to sleep, guards closed and locked the huge iron gates, opening them after sunrise, locking them before dusk.

"That'll stop her," Scallin said. "I told the guards just to keep her outside when she tried to come back in. She can come in during visiting hours just like anyone, but no baby buggie, and no damned noise."

Chet heard from Billie Bob that it worked one day only. The fence that fronted the cemetery extended from end to end, but it protected only one side of the grounds. Entry could be gained from the back of the property.

"She's back," Scallin then told Chet angrily. "We had a burial yesterday and they said she was up in the graves singing all through the service, raising hell like bad asses was after her, and she was about to die." He shook his head. "Do you think she'd pay any mind to a law suit?"

"I don't know," Chet said truthfully. "I guess if you got a court order you might have to get a judge to put her in jail to make it stick."

"Bad publicity again?" Scallin asked, watching him.

Chet shrugged.

"Maybe someone from your old cemetery group put her up to this?" Scallin asked calculatingly.

"I don't think so. The head man moved to Orlando. The rest are pretty old."

"We had special board of directors meeting last night. Someone mentioned we might turn Billy Bob loose on her to tear up her stuff. Before we do that I want you to go and talk with her one more time."

"Okay," Chet said. He kept his face set stern. "Maybe we could just ignore her for a few weeks. She'll quit soon now. It's just a fixation."

"How do you know she'll quit?"

"I know. She never stays long past September's end and the full moon. She believes them guys that's buried where she does her rituals want to roam every four years come end of summer."

"I don't give a damn what some nutcase believes. It's your job to tell her she can't come on the premises except like other visitors. She's *your* relative and she ought to listen to you."

"She never has," Chet answered. He saw Scallin was angry at him and added: "But I'll sure go right up and see her, sir."

"Yeah, do that." Scallin thought for a moment. "And, to make sure she listens this time, you take Billy Bob along. Maybe with him beside you in his uniform and looking mean, she'll get our message."

Billy Bob, squat and strong, sat grinning his perpetual, frozen grin beside Chet in the Jeep. Chet had heard the stories about Billy Bob and an old jungle war. Billy Bob, home with a chest full of medals from 'Nam, had joined the police first, but that had only lasted until his first bloody arrest. Since then he'd worked here and there, done prison time for assault, and now he had a new job wearing a uniform again.

"We got to be gentle with her," Chet cautioned. "She's old." He remembered being young and harem scarem, running wild in the project. Some people there had feared the old lady, some had laughed at her. He had only wanted to be old enough to escape her.

"I think you look exactly like her, Chet."

Chet stared forward without replying. *Long ago it had been running from crazy orders and rules.*

Elizabeth did ritual around the two suspect graves. She'd laid out the crucifix and made marks on the ground and she

85

looked first to one grave and then to the other. Leaves and grass lay on the graves.

"Onalla, Umgowe, power to us all," she chanted.

Billy Bob moved close, leaned down, and thunked the nightstick hard against the crucifix.

"Stop, crazy woman."

"Please Mr. Billy Bob, let me do the talking to her."

Billy Bob nodded. "Okay, you do that, Chet. You and her got color and blood in common." He was white.

"They ain't going to let you do this," Chet said. "You can come in at visiting hours, but no noise, no rituals."

Billy Bob thunked the crucifix harder. "Better listen, old witch." He nodded down at her. "I followed you. I know your routine. I know where you live down there in the project. You leave and you stay gone. Otherwise I'll come back if you come back. I'll bring along Mr. Scallin. He's the high boss. We ain't going to law you or let you talk to nosy reporters. What we'll do is burn your junk and hurt you where folks can't see the hurt. I'll be the one to do it." He looked down at her for a long moment. "You hear?"

Chet tried to read old eyes as Hattie stared up at Billy Bob.

"I hear," she said finally.

Billy Bob thunked the crucifix one more time.

"You going to leave?"

"I guess. Go back to the project." She looked at Chet. "You for this?"

"I work here, but I ain't going to see you hurt. I promise you that."

"Eat spit's what you do."

Billy Bob smiled all the way back to the office. Chet knew at least a part of the smile was aimed at him.

"Mr. Scallin will tell the board at special meeting tonight how you helped out," he said. "You just about the same purple color as that old lady."

"I guess."

Billy Bob laughed. "And you was going to stop me?"

"Going to try."

Billy Bob laughed some more.

When he got off work Chet parked his aging Plymouth at the project. He watched through the night to make sure the board sent no one to hurt the old lady.

He saw fights, drug transactions, and domestic disturbances in the project. Once a man came yelling into the street and fired a shotgun into the sky. A couple of police cars came past afterwards, driving fast, windows up.

Quiet night.

Most of the people in the project, black and white, had no money, little to eat, and not a single dream left.

In the hazy morning, when Chet arrived at the cemetery, the office was silent. The gate stood unlocked. It was too early for any of the boiler room phone employees. They arrived at noon and worked until eight at night.

Chet sat at his small desk and thought on what needed doing on this day. He was tired from his night vigil.

Perhaps it was time to just quit. He wondered if he could get another job. Could be it was time to find out. He had a little money put by. *Move somewhere.*

Scallin didn't come.

The phone rang a few times. Chet answered and kept things going. Scallin had been late before. He drank.

At nine o'clock diggers came and Chet got his spade and accompanied them up to the old cemetery to open two gravesites. The diggers had a big Ford truck so he rode with them. One of the secretaries had arrived by then so there was someone to answer the office phone.

The day was lovely with only a hint of fall in it. *A good day to be alive.*

Hattie sat beside her graves. She saw Chet and the workers when they alighted from the Ford truck and she waved.

Chet, who had worried about her, waved back. She must have entered early. She knelt on the ground and smiled up at the morning sun. A yellow-leaved tree shaded the area where the two men lay buried.

Chet showed the gravediggers where the plots were that had to be opened and used his spade to help them start.

He could hear Hattie singing gibberish.

One of the white diggers watched her apprehensively.

"That old lady really gets right to it," he said. "Makes the insides of me shiver."

Chet nodded. He looked around to see if Billie Bob or any other guards were near.

Hattie's morning ritual was soon completed and she became quiet again. Chet saw she was watching him. He waved again at her and she beckoned.

He walked to where she sat.

She smiled at him. "Good morning, sweetie."

"Yes'm. I kept a watch at your place last night. That one man's plain mean."

"I seen you there before I slipped out," she said. "Bad men wash off me like Monday laundry. I never had no trouble. And I apologize for talking down to you. You're you and I'm me. You don't believe and I do. We've known that a long time. Since before you run off from me."

"Sure," he said, watching her, feeling an old, lost feeling of remembered love. She had comforted and cared for him when he was small and afraid of many things. That still meant something.

Something seemed odd about the cemetery scene, but he

couldn't figure it out for a long moment.

And then he did.

"Were you in the graveyard during the night?" he asked.

She smiled and nodded. "Full service. They was crawling and wanting booger bad to get at Ned, but I put them to rest."

"Did Billy Bob and Mr. Scallin see you?"

She smiled again.

"You must have worked things out with them?"

One more nod. "All worked out. Billy Bob hit at me with his stick. Once."

Chet looked at her and the earth that surrounded her and realized what was different. Now, instead of just the two graves with the injured crucifix between them, there were four graves.

Four graves crowded together, two of them fresher than the two old graves, and spread only with a carpet of heaped leaves. No headstones.

She lowered her face close to the ground, listening. "The new ones movin' down there." She smiled upward.

Chet's hands felt cold in the morning heat.

"I wish you'd come back home, sweetie. I'm old. I need someone to help. I got to teach someone before I go on."

Chet watched, rubbing his hands, now as cold as ice cubes.

"I'll die mighty soon." She then chanted very softly, "Onallo, Umgowe . . ."

One of the gravediggers blew the horn as they departed and Chet waved them on.

He had no one. He considered things and his hands grew warmer.

As he watched, he saw the ground move. He felt sudden triumph at what she'd accomplished, and a deepening curiosity about it. When the worker's truck had vanished he took his spade and struck the grave hard. From someplace deep he heard a scream and so he smacked the grave again and then smacked the other one until all hint of motion stopped.

So long Scallin. So long Billy Bob.

"Come home," she said.

He sighed. "Yes, great grandmother."

Killer Scent

The small man came into my courthouse office in the afternoon just after yet another report of *someone* spotting Joe Ringer. The man waited patiently while I ordered a car dispatched to the sighting area.

"Could I speak with you privately, Sheriff?" he then asked politely.

I examined him. He was so thin that he could be called emaciated. I thought him to be about my age, early forties. His handshake was soft and so somehow reserved. He wore rumpled, conservative clothes, thick glasses, and sported a small beard. He looked all right, but my sensitive nose smelled desperation and death, and I was distrustful of him. Most men trust something. I trust my nose.

"Edward Allen Reynolds," he said, introducing himself.

I nodded shortly. My long dead father once told me never to believe well of anyone who used three names.

"Sheriff Spain," I replied. "Things are busy. If you came to talk to Joe Ringer I'm sorry to report he somehow walked away from my jail last night."

He looked stricken. "I'd like to have talked to him, but not for what you probably think. My only interest is how he got to your town, Sheriff." He gave me a sharp look. "How'd he manage to just walk away?"

"If I knew, I'd be a happier man," I said, still not sure of his intentions. I'd thought at first he might be another reporter like the many who'd appeared in Crossville like wolves drawn to bait when we'd picked up Joe Ringer.

"If you aren't a reporter then what are you?" I asked.

"I'm a psychology professor at a small college in the East, but I'm on Sabbatical just now. If you'd like to check on me, you can call the head of the psychology department at your state university. He'll tell you I'm bona fide."

I considered doing that for a moment and decided against it. "I'm very busy," I said pointedly. "This is an election year." I tried to read his eyes behind their thick glasses, but nothing solid happened. There was only the faint smell to him of hurt or injury or desperation. "If you want to talk more about Joe Ringer I can recommend my deputy, Chick Gaitlin. He spotted Ringer in the bus station and arrested him." Gaitlin had been very popular with the disappointed newsmen all day.

"I think it's you I need to talk with, Sheriff," he said, lowering his voice. "I've got a theory that Joe Ringer was lured to your town for some reason I don't understand."

I smiled a little at that. "I've got an election opponent who's screaming all over the county today about my inefficiency, and I've got an escaped multiple murderer. I don't need wild theories. I do need to find Joe Ringer. Take your theories to the press. Perhaps they'd like them. They've turned Ringer into a folk hero instead of a cold killer."

"Please let me have a few moments of your time in private," he said. He looked around. The gum-chewing deputy who was operating the radio was listening curiously. I'd heard he was the one who'd leaked things to my opponent all through the campaign. He'd probably been promised more rank and a better job after I was voted out. I knew he disliked me because I'd put him on the radio. Maybe he was the leak, maybe not. Election years make for chronic paranoia. I'd spent a lot of time getting where I was. I didn't plan to lose it. I had no wife, no family. I had only the job and the opportunities it brought.

"All right. Come into my private parlor, Edward Allen Reynolds," I said. I got up from the littered desk and led him into my dingy private office, closing the door behind us.

"First off I need to know how Joe Ringer got here?" he asked.

"Routinely enough. On a bus. A deputy saw him get off a bus and picked him up at the station. That was yesterday morning."

"But why would Ringer appear here? Why to this town, of all places?"

"Why not? Crossville's a nice town. Thirty thousand plus and growing. Industry, power, and farming. Read our Chamber of Commerce handouts."

"A lot of trails I've followed may have ended in your Crossville in the past few years, Sheriff. Did you ever hear of one Peter Green?"

"No," I said. I had, but I wanted Reynolds to talk, not me.

"I traced him here. He has a sister in Florida. I started there. He was a heavy suspect there and in some other states on maybe a dozen rape murders. She showed me his picture. Handsome young man who made his living as a long-distance trucker. Somehow young women died almost every time he was very long around a town. His sister told me he came to Crossville because of a very good job offer from some firm called Multiple Trucking Incorporated. I checked them out earlier today. There isn't any company by that name around here and never has been. This sister hasn't heard from him since he left Florida. I've reason to suspect she never will again."

"I've sure never heard of the company," I said stolidly. "And I've lived all of my life around here. But so what?"

He shrugged. "Only that Green's missing in your town. I

ran down one more certain, a construction worker named William Kole. I believe he killed for kicks, getting some kind of sick joy out of it, a butcher boy. He came out of Pennsylvania originally, but lived in San Francisco until he came here some months back. He was tried once in California for murder, but there wasn't enough evidence to make it stick. After the trial he moved here to work on your new power plant. I've got a copy of his work application. But when they tried to call him for work he'd disappeared. No one's seen him since." He shook his head, very intent, a man obsessed with his quest. "There have been some others I can't document as well yet. They apparently wound up here, but I can't prove it." He nodded positively. "I think they did. So I'll continue to check."

"All this is most interesting," I said, "but right now I'm a political candidate with a bad problem. I need to find Joe Ringer or start looking for a new job after the first of the year. And I like this job and also like to think I'm competent at it."

"I've heard around that you are, Sheriff. All I want is permission to stick close. I think Joe Ringer may have also been lured here. If I can talk with him then maybe I can find out exactly how."

"I don't need or want anyone in the way."

"A trade then. I've an idea or two about where Ringer might be found." He gave me a quick look. "All based on my research. I need to know something else first. Could he have been aided in his escape?"

"It's possible," I said, not liking to tell it. "He got away right at shift change time. He came out for a call after talking with his court-appointed attorney. Somehow he then just walked away."

"Who'd he call?"

I hesitated, not knowing how much to tell him. "We don't

listen to prisoner phone calls."

"Come now, Sheriff Spain. Let's be truthful with each other. Ringer's a man suspected of at least thirty murders, men, women, children. He's a professional burglar and robber who enters homes and coldly kills anyone he finds inside, steals only the untraceables, and moves on. He's bright and careful and merciless. He's never been well caught. He's been tried twice and found innocent. I've got to think you cut a few corners on him. Who'd he call?"

I shook my head.

"What if I could name some names and one of them was who he called?"

"I'm not here to play games with you, Mr. Reynolds," I said, worried a little now.

"It's Professor Reynolds, really. Don't you want to find out what's happening in your town? What if Joe Ringer was lured here?"

"For what reason?" I asked.

"To be killed," he said.

"Then good riddance," I said, out of temper. "That won't bother me as long as it doesn't keep me from winning reelection."

"Nor me," he agreed softly. "But your problem is complicated because you've never found the bodies of any of the others, Sheriff. You won't find Ringer either unless you level with me. Please, let me give you my names."

I nodded reluctantly. He seemed sincere. But somehow I could still scent death on him.

He dug a piece of paper out of his pocket and began reading. I stopped him on the fourth name. Quinn Cowper. A farmer, a raiser of beef cattle. I knew him well.

"How'd you get your names?" I asked curiously.

"My list contains the names of everyone in your town that

I ran onto in my little investigation. Cowper isn't the name I ran onto most. That one I won't share with you now. But apparently Cowper's the name we should be watching to catch Joe Ringer." He nodded at me. "Shall we go?"

I hesitated and then nodded. I led him out of the courthouse and past the old men who continually whittled their sticks on the wall. Some of them nodded at me, others did not. *Election year.*

Cowper lived north, down an old gravel road, miles from the interstate. I took Reynolds, but no one else.

We hid the marked car out of sight and walked up a hill. I carried my best high-powered rifle.

From the top of the hill you could see most of the Cowper place. There was a ramshackle old house, a fallen-in barn, and a few other out-of-repair outbuildings. There was a good fence tented at the top with barbed wire strands. We repair the fences first in my part of the country.

We sat in the dry, cool fall grass and watched. There was no immediate sign of life from the house, no movement, no smoke.

"I'll bet your man is there," Reynolds whispered beside me.

"Maybe, maybe not. I don't know why he would be there, and I still don't completely understand your interest. Why are you here?"

He gave me a strange look. "I need to know how it works. How does Cowper get multiple murderers to come here, perhaps die here? How does he know or recognize them, contact them, entice them?"

I sniffed the air. Soon the cold days would come.

"Why do you care?"

He gave me a peculiar look, and I knew I wasn't getting it

all. "I'm a psychologist. All my life I've had some minor interest in the criminal mind. In the last few years that interest has been forcibly turned to mass murderers and multiple killers as a class. There seem suddenly to be more of them, as if because more people are being born, there needs to be a doubling or tripling of their ratio among us. I've got some figures . . ."

"Forcibly turned?" I asked, stopping him.

He held up a paper-thin hand. "Someone's come onto the porch down there. See?"

I looked at the farmhouse. There was someone.

"Is that Joe Ringer?" he asked.

The man below moved into better light. It was Ringer. I could see his pinched face and cold eyes. I nodded. "That's him."

He shook his head and whispered, "Not the one."

"That's Ringer," I said, perplexed. "Not which one?"

"Let's go down after him," Reynolds said, ignoring my question. He had a bad habit of doing that, and so puzzled me.

"Wait awhile," I said. "He looks as if he's waiting for someone. I'd like to know who." I wasn't ready to retake Ringer yet. I had too many questions unanswered about Reynolds.

"He's probably waiting for Cowper," Reynolds said.

"No, not Cowper," I said positively. "I know Cowper well, know he's in a hospital in a city forty miles from here. He was also there last night. I checked that out earlier." I smiled. "I thought maybe you might know who else it could be that Ringer's waiting for?"

He shook his head. "I truly don't. I swear it. We wait, then?"

"For a while. Someone helped him out, someone

answered his call. I wish I knew who. What with civil rights, the Miranda case, and Supreme Court decisions on wiretaps, I can't let my deputies take chances on bending the rules these days."

"But maybe you took a chance?"

I shrugged noncommittally. I pointed downward through the red and yellow fall foliage, somehow wanting to move things along. "There's a cattle tunnel under the road. We'll go through it and get closer."

"Maybe we ought to do like you said and stay right here until we spot his helper," he said, hesitant now. "We've surely not been seen so far. He might see us if we start moving in on him."

"I'm running this show, Professor. I want to wait for your mystery man, but I've decided to do that waiting up close. So follow or stay here. Up to you."

He followed. We stayed behind trees and bushes and moved carefully. In a while we were within fifty yards of the house in a copse of trees. Joe Ringer, in the meantime, had disappeared back inside the house, but I could see movement now and then when he came to the front window and watched the road.

Insects whined about us voraciously as we waited out the long afternoon. Cars intermittently passed on the gravel road that paralleled the front fence. Professor Reynolds stiffened in anticipation each time one approached, but always the cars continued onward.

When the sun was almost down I made Reynolds move even closer to the house. Still no one came. Joe Ringer, now more confident as the light dimmed, came back onto the porch and impatiently watched the road.

"I'm going to have to go ahead and take him," I whispered

finally. "It's getting dark. He could get away from us into the night."

"I need to know who he's waiting for," Reynolds whispered back angrily. "Remember that I found him for you."

I shook my head. I leveled my rifle and got Ringer in its sights.

"Stop right there, Ringer."

"Sheriff?" he called.

"Don't move."

He did what I'd thought he'd do and moved. He threw himself to the left and pulled desperately at his waistband. I bounced one errant shot through a window and hit him squarely with two more.

"No," Reynolds called, stricken. "No! I needed him."

"So did I," I said softly, thinking about my coming election. I moved cautiously to the porch, Reynolds following. Ringer lay unmoving. I'd aimed for his head. I foot-turned him. Already he smelled dead. A small caliber pistol lay beside him. I wrapped it in a handkerchief.

"You might have taken him without killing him," Reynolds accused.

I shook my head. "Not without taking bad chances. And not with you along. You saw his reaction when I called out. He went for his gun. He tried to get away."

"Where'd he get a gun?"

"Maybe the house," I said. "Maybe he found it inside the house."

I searched the body while he watched. I found the familiar note with Cowper's number on it, directions crudely printed to the farmhouse.

Reynolds said despondently, "Whoever it was could have been waiting out there for full dark, Sheriff. You've scared him off for good now." He shook his head. "This won't stop me. I'm going to go on looking. Someone in your town somehow got Ringer to come here. Someone didn't want him caught. *Someone.*" He watched me.

I knew he was adding too many numbers in his head, and so I aimed the rifle at him.

He nodded, sure now. "Your name was on my list also. Top of the list."

I shook my head. "I've never had to kill anyone other than one of them. Cowper's my cousin. I take care of this place sometimes for him. I'm not going to be able to take a chance on your running around, talking. I've slept good until now. I'm thinking you'll keep me awake nights, Professor. I don't hate you like I do them."

He gave me an unafraid smile.

"How do you do it? Tell me how you spot them. How do you get them here?"

I shook my head. "I don't know where it came from, but I've had a very sensitive sense of smell all my life. A gift. A gift of smell. People like Ringer and Peter Green and the several others planted out there in ailing cousin Cowper's fields have an odor I can smell." I nodded. "I smell them out, acrid and pungent. It hurts me inside when I smell them. I got it first when I was only a kid. I wanted to kill that first one who smelled so bad, but I didn't because I was only about eight years old. Then, when I was deputying for Frank Stickney, we caught one who'd killed five people, and he smelled just like that first one. All he got from the law was thirty days for vagrancy because we couldn't prove a thing on the murders, and he just laughed at us when we asked him questions about them. When he was released I got him and put him in deep here."

"You smell them?" he asked.

I nodded. "Now, every year I go on vacation, plus the job

100

takes me places. There aren't any more around here, but last year I was in San Francisco and this year it's supposed to be New York. I tell the police in the cities that I've got a man supposed to be in their city. I ask where's a good place for someone hiding to hang around. Sometimes I just wander. And you're right. There seem to be more of them all the time." I smiled. "It's not hard to find someone who has the smell, sometimes more than one someone."

"And so you kill them?" he asked, somehow eager to hear about it.

"Not then. I find out what I can about my candidates. I do it carefully. Most of them are as wary as old foxes and also very bright. Sometimes, after I learn what I can about him or her, for there are females of the species, I can figure a way to get them here, a ruse, a subterfuge. Joe Ringer fancied himself a writer. I found him and sent him a letter offering to publish his stuff. I paid his way here. It was just bad luck my deputy saw him and arrested him in the bus depot. So I had to let him escape. It was easy enough. I wrote him a note to meet me here and smuggled it to him. I intercepted his call."

"And Peter Green?"

"He came to manage my trucking company."

He nodded, apparently delighted. I leveled the gun reluctantly.

"Not yet, please. You need to hear a few more important things before you decide on killing me." His eyes sparkled behind their thick glass shields. For the first time they seemed alive. "Your deputies saw me leave with you for one thing."

"You tragically got in the line of fire," I said. "That's one of the reasons I missed with one shot. A sheriff doesn't have to answer many questions, especially with Joe Ringer dead." I shook my head. "Somehow you knew he was here and you led me to him. You died. I'll make you a hero, Professor, if that's any consolation."

He nodded approval. "That might work, but I've been tracking multiple murderers for a while. Others, all over the country, know about me and my fixation. I've never been as open with any of them as I was with you, but I never suspected any of them as I did you. I don't think any one of them took me seriously. You can hope not, anyway. I'll hope so, too. But someone could get very serious if I wound up dead."

That was something to think on, and I pondered it.

He waited patiently.

"I'm sorry. I don't have a choice. If I can win my election then, with luck, I'll have another four years of hunting them. And somehow I have to hunt them. Maybe I'm different, maybe I'm their specific for dying. I hate them as they hate us." I nodded at him. "Sometimes I think they're mutants, the coming race for earth. I've thought on it lots. Maybe they came along to wipe us out, take our places, be the survivors of the cities, mercilessly preying on each other after we're gone." My voice trembled a little.

"Easy, Sheriff Spain," he said soothingly. "I told you I got into multiple murderers forcibly. Three years ago a man got into my house when I was away. He killed my daughter first. She was ten years old, quite pretty, already a small woman. He did things to her after she was dead. He then beat and raped my wife and left her for dead. She did die, but not for a long, hideous time, not before she told us—me—what he looked like. When my family died I also mostly died." He smiled without any humor at all. "Out there in your field would you perhaps have a man with a white patch of hair on the right side of his head, six feet or so tall, early thirties, hawk-featured?"

I shook my head. "No one like that. Not yet."

"I see," he said, disappointed.

I waited. I'd lowered the gun.

He asked, "Did you ever think how much more efficiently you could work this if you had someone who knew psychology, who could figure out ways to bring even the cleverest of them within reach? A trained person?"

I considered the possibilities. There were hundreds of them out there, maybe thousands, enough for a lifetime.

"You could help me live again," he said softly, deciding for me. "I tracked you down to be your assistant."

The Home

Shelby's second heart attack came during a trial in which he was defending a man named Blandon on a jewel burglary. He remembered the crushing pain, falling, then blackness.

When he was allowed to leave the hospital, it was only upon his promise to move to a nursing home.

Shelby sold his condo and appointed his bank to handle his affairs.

He then prepared to die. He found that it took very little effort and was, except for recurring dark-of-the-night sweats when he was sure he'd not live to see morning again, boring.

He was sixty-seven and he still seemed healthy enough after he'd recovered from the attack. There was angina pain and shortness of breath, but that was it as far as overt symptoms went. His doctor explained to him that his heart was *insufficient* and that he needed a place where he could have constant medical attention available. So, a nursing home.

At times, thinking about his bad heart made Shelby smile. There were lawyers, particularly criminal prosecutors, who'd have sworn on a pile of religious tracts that he was heartless, lawyers he'd crushed by cleverness in closing argument or by vicious cross-examination of unsure prosecution witnesses. He'd mostly defended persons accused of murder, but he'd taken other criminal cases when there were no murder cases to be tried. He'd been an advocate's advocate. He'd taken only cases where he believed the accused innocent, losing some, winning a lot.

He'd been the best, but now there'd be no more trials. His

heart condition made it impossible. The tension of a trial, the open warfare wherein a client might lose his freedom or life, had been what he lived for. Without the courtroom he felt useless. *And old—finally old.*

The nursing home was named Eden. It sat on a hill in the middle of wooded acreage ten miles distant from the city where Shelby had practiced. It had been a private estate, but when it had been sold for a nursing home the mansion had been modernized. There was a high, barbed fence around the property and an armed guard at the closed gate. *Safe.*

There was a separate building near the gate for visitors, but visitors seldom came. Eden specialized in patients who didn't have close relatives. The literature given to those interested in the home was frank about it. "We want people who need us. We want to be your family."

Shelby had selected the place after reading various competing tracts and then had been interviewed by Mr. Hoskins from the home before being "accepted."

"Ours is a quiet place," Mr. Hoskins had warned. "We control all visitation. We also don't permit our patients to travel outside the nursing home. We have our own inhouse medical staff and we would expect your doctor to turn your complete medical file over to our people. Our staff is the best in the field of geriatric medicine. Would anything I've said be a problem? If so, we can stop now."

"I doubt it," Shelby said. His own doctor didn't like him. The doctor's house had been burglarized once and he'd told Shelby tartly he had no use for lawyers who protected criminals.

Mr. Hoskins looked approvingly at Shelby's written application. "I see you list no family. Understand again that we limit visitation to once every other week with relatives. All visitation is carried out in an area adjacent to the home under strict supervision. We can't have visitors upsetting our patients."

Shelby shook his head. "I've two cousins, but I've not heard from either of them in years. I never married. Never found the time. There'd be no visitors."

"You were a lawyer. Were you with a large firm?"

"Single practitioner," Shelby said. "I was ordered to shut my office down after my last attack."

"You seem to have the necessary finances to pay us," Hoskins continued, his tone favorable.

"Yes," Shelby said. "I can pay you. Your place isn't as expensive as many. Yet, except for your visitation rules, it seems the best. How do you manage that?"

"We're privately endowed. Certain of our patients have left us their estates or a part of their estates as a reward for the care we gave them in their declining years. That's why we're careful about admissions." Mr. Hoskins smiled a little. "During your stay with us, if you find our facilities satisfactory, we would expect you to consider a gift to the home upon your eventual demise."

"Is that required?" Shelby asked, not liking that part.

"Certainly not," Hoskins answered reprovingly. "But you should remember that your care is being partially paid for by those who resided at the home before you. We ask only that you consider such a bequest once you've experienced the care we provide."

It sounded reasonable. Shelby examined Hoskins. The nursing-home administrator seemed above reproach. His clothes were expensive and neat, he was fiftyish, and he wore hornrims. All his movements were precise. A jury would believe him. He vaguely reminded Shelby of a child molester he had defended (and lost) years back. Very proper.

They shook hands and it was settled. Shelby signed a

penalty-clause contract.

Mr. Hoskins smiled as he was leaving. "We'll see you soon," he said. "Have a good day."

And so Shelby moved to Eden.

The first patient he met was a one-time client. His name was Julian Kay and Shelby had defended him twenty years back when Kay's wife had died under suspicious but ultimately unprovable (at least as far as Kay was concerned) circumstances. Arsenic poisoning. The State's difficulties had been in showing that Kay had administered the poison to his wife when tests ordered by Shelby showed Kay himself had traces of arsenic in his own body. Shelby knew that those who used arsenic as a poison often managed to accidentally ingest some of it themselves. He suspected Kay's wife had tried to poison Kay and botched it. That was his winning trial tactic.

Kay had the next room. He sat upright in bed. "How are you?" Shelby asked solicitously when Hoskins introduced them.

Kay ignored the question. He watched Shelby. "Devil," he said. "Devil!" He shook with agitation.

Hoskins drew Shelby away. "He makes no sense some days. He's had a series of small strokes. He's been here for a long time."

"How long?"

Hoskins made a vague gesture. "A long time. Years. Why do you ask?"

Shelby shrugged. He'd lost track of Kay soon after the trial. The man had been peculiar. But he'd sworn his innocence and Shelby had believed him.

At times thereafter Shelby would nod in at Kay from the door without receiving a response. Kay's color was bad and he was about fifty pounds lighter than Shelby remembered him. Shelby heard one of the pretty nurses say Kay was "on his deathbed." Sometimes Shelby could hear him groaning at night. He also heard doctors in the room working on Kay and saw attendants pushing complicated life support machines into his room. But Kay lived on.

There were things Shelby didn't agree with in the home's routine. The food was good enough, but it wasn't a coronary diet. It was high-fat food—meat and gravy, and rich desserts at noon and at night. For breakfast it was eggs with bacon or sausage, heavily buttered toast, pancakes, and sweet rolls, served leisurely and late. It was the kind of food Shelby had wanted but not allowed himself to eat outside, after the first attack. (Meals were served on china with heavy silverware, a budding rose in a vase on the bed tray, by a smiling attendant—female and pretty for the male patients, handsome and muscular for the female patients.)

The doctor assigned to Shelby, Dr. Cart, seemed vaguely familiar to him. Shelby asked him about the diet and he spoke of "good" triglycerides and cholesterol and "bad" ones, and of a secret Eden food-treatment formula. He took Shelby's pulse and listened intently to the faulty heart. "You're doing well," he said. He then marked a special diet for him on his card, which he told Shelby was optional if a patient worried about his diet and requested another.

"We're all born with ailing hearts," he joked. "It stops, we stop. Sleep. Watch TV. See what a fine set you have? Trust us. Relax."

Shelby nodded, thinking the humor unfunny, at least to a man with a heart as "insufficient" as his.

Thereafter, sometimes the special diet came, sometimes it didn't. When it did come, it was unappetizing, as if the fine Eden cooks had thrown it on the plate in disgust. He didn't complain again about the food, and gradually the regular diet returned to full-time status.

Shelby did feel well, but he'd felt that way before both heart attacks. He slept nine or ten hours a night. He tried to keep from gaining weight by eating sparsely. He looked in vain for any sort of exercise facility to burn up calories and keep his aging muscles fit.

"Don't you have exercise facilities here?" he asked the doctor.

Dr. Cart sniffed. "No. We decided against an exercise area. We believe that our patients benefit more from rest than exercise. You're not a boy anymore, Mr. Shelby. You'll live longer doing things our way."

"But surely some mild exercise should be beneficial?"

"I'm not in total disagreement," Dr. Cart conceded. "You're a bit younger than our usual patient. I'll allow you to improvise."

Shelby improvised and walked. If there was angina pain or shortness of breath he stopped for a while, then walked some more.

He observed that a high percentage of the patients at Eden ran from mildly fat to clearly obese. When he commented on it, Dr. Cart frowned. "You were a lawyer outside, Mr. Shelby, not a doctor. Leave the practice of medicine to us. Fat isn't automatically fatal."

There was a decent library, which kept Shelby from becoming a TV addict like so many of the other patients.

When fall became winter, more of the walks he took were confined to inside the mansion. He was allowed to roam everywhere except the staff areas. The staff door was kept locked, but now and then when the door was open he caught a glimpse of rich draperies, lush furniture, and a hanging chandelier. Shelby guessed those rooms had been the central part of the original mansion. Some nights he heard sounds of revelry from within. Early in the morning he could hear the staff breakfasting together before the patients were served.

The kitchen, the surgery, and the intensive-care rooms were also in that area and out of bounds. Once, during an evening walk, he examined the lock on the staff door. It was a simple one. Blandon, the accused burglar and jewel thief Shelby had last represented, had taught him about locks, after convincing Shelby he was innocent "this time." Shelby thought he could open the staff lock given the time plus some tools in his manicure set and wallet.

The home was becoming an easy life. Late breakfast, noon lunch, early dinner. Read, sleep, and walk. Outside, snow fell. Christmas and New Year's came. The staff held a sedate party for the patients and a wild one for themselves behind the staff door.

Shelby counted staff—doctors, nurses, attendants, maintenance people. There were a great many. None seemed to work very hard. Several times Shelby could have sworn he smelled scotch on Cart's breath. And the night attendant in Shelby's area seemed to sleep better than Shelby.

Eden had a sixty-patient capacity. Multiplying what he paid for his own care times sixty did not add to a figure Shelby found impressive as revenue. The remainder must come from endowments.

The home was extremely quiet. Shelby saw the doctors, nurses, and attendants doling out pills for nerves, for sleep, for everything—pills and smiles—and decided it was quiet because so many of the old people were heavily doped. It was a great place to eat and sleep and die.

But what if you weren't ready to die?

One night, out of boredom, he tested his burglar-client's instructions and picked open the lock of one of the medicine chests, using a sharp cuticle pick from his manicure set. He managed it silently and easily in the darkness while the night attendant snored. The chest was stocked with tranquilizers and sedatives. A locked compartment inside yielded to further probing. There were things he didn't recognize. Some of the bottles were marked with skull and crossbones. Others were strong sedatives or narcotics. Bottles of both types had been opened. Shelby didn't think that unusual. He knew doctors used all sorts of medicines and that some poisons did not kill if given in careful doses. He closed the chest back up.

He'd always been a light sleeper, but now he found himself sleeping well and long. Maybe there was something in the cocoa. It was oversweet, full of whipped cream, and had a slightly metallic aftertaste. At first he drank it, but later he poured it into a large flowerpot beside his bed. Then he would prowl Eden's dark halls until dawn. He was restless and, for the first time in his life, lonely.

Hoskins, the administrator, talked with him in his office one day. By that time Shelby had made a few acquaintances. There was a fat old man he played chess with. The man had suffered a stroke and lost most of his ability to speak and all movement on his right side, but he could still use his left hand to move chessmen. He was an expert player. They kept the old man, whose name was Detmen, heavily tranquilized, but Detmen seemed resistant to the medicine and could function around it. Most of the people in the home were lumps. Detmen was refreshing.

His movements with the left hand were quick and snakelike. "Gotchee," he'd say. "Checkmay." Then he'd grin lopsidedly. A fine old man who'd been an architect.

Detmen didn't like Dr. Cart. "Dite duck," he'd mutter darkly when Cart was near. Shelby finally figured that he was trying to say, "Diet doc."

There were three elderly ladies who invited Shelby to play bridge. They painted their lips and flirted with him outrageously, tittering at each other behind their cards. He was gallant with them and tried not to trump their aces. Then one of them, Laura Shannon, died one night and that ended the bridge sessions. The two survivors seemed not to know each other afterward. Shelby thought they might be getting added doses of tranquilizer from their doctors. Or maybe Laura Shannon had been the glue that held the bridge games together.

He asked Dr. Cart about it. "What did Laura Shannon die of?"

Cart pursed his lips. "She had many problems. High blood pressure, a bad heart, and diabetes. She was over eighty. People don't live forever, Mr. Shelby."

"She was the most active of all the bridge players," Shelby said. "She seemed perfectly all right to me."

"Maybe hyperactivity helped speed her death," Dr. Cart answered reasonably. "That's something you might think about, Mr. Shelby. Are you walking too much? Are you too busy? Our attendants say you wander around a great deal, even at night."

"I'm restless," Shelby explained. "I need the exercise."

Detmen died as Shelby started his fifth month in the home. It was during an in-home operation Cart told Shelby had been intended to open up the large artery running from the heart to the brain. Detmen had said nothing to Shelby about any operation.

No more chess or bridge. Just walking.

Sometimes he caught the attendants watching him as he prowled the darkened halls. Sometimes he thought they used care in what they said to him and how.

I'm paranoid, he thought.

With the two people he'd liked most at Eden dead, Shelby tried to watch the soaps during the day but couldn't stand them. Instead, he watched the snow beyond his window and dreamed of green grass and outdoor walks.

Hoskins smiled, interrupting Shelby's walk, and led him to his office.

"Are you enjoying your life here, Mr. Shelby?"

"It's adequate," Shelby said.

"No more than that?" Hoskins asked, pouting a little.

Shelby relented. "It's nice." He tried a bit of sarcasm. "Very quiet. It's hard to become acquainted with people. They die."

Hoskins nodded piously. "Death is only a part of life. We must all face it sooner or later. This is a home for old, sick people. We keep them alive and happy as long as we can."

"Yes." Shelby had been thinking a great deal about Detmen. "But Mr. Detmen might have lived if he hadn't been operated on."

Hoskins shrugged. "He wanted to be better, to be well again. Unfortunately, it wasn't to be. He died on the operating table. It was a shame." He leaned forward. "May I talk with you on something of importance?"

Shelby nodded assent.

"We've had our lawyers prepare our form will plus a codicil to an already existing will showing bequests to Eden. The bequest figure in the forms is what we recommend to someone in your financial bracket without close relatives. Of course, you can devise any figure you want, less or more. We'd like you to examine the forms."

Shelby said all right.

Hoskins handed him a sheaf of papers and shook his hand moistly. "May I call on you in a week or so?"

"You said there was no obligation?"

"Absolutely." Mr. Hoskins smiled. He reminded Shelby of a minister he'd defended for the murder of his sister, a man who swore on a Bible he had not done the murder. Shelby had dressed him all in black and had him carry and read his Bible in court while the trial proceeded. The jury had come back in an hour with a verdict of not guilty.

Shelby took the will back to his room, examined it, and shoved it in a drawer. His own will was made. His money was to be shared by a youth club he admired and his university. He saw no reason to change it.

He told Hoskins his decision a week later. The man inclined his head. "Perhaps you'll change your mind as time passes," he said. "Some do. I hope you'll continue to consider it."

Shelby found himself watching what went on around him more closely. Having made it known that he would leave the home no money in his will, he wondered what would happen.

The food and service remained good. But he realized that someone shadowed him those nights he walked the darkened halls. And it seemed even harder to stay awake now than before he had started to dump the hot chocolate.

No one came to visit, but although Shelby expected no one a fragile hope remained. He had a few legal friends outside. One might come. His secretary of many years had moved to Florida when the office closed. He asked about calling out to his bank and was refused. When he insisted, Dr. Cart came to see him.

"We don't let you do that," he said. "You're here because you ruined your health with worry and work. Now we take care of all that for you. Every month we send an itemized bill to your bank, along with a statement of your physical condition." He shook his head and again Shelby caught a faint odor of scotch. "Relax. Use the home. Enjoy us."

"I only want to talk to the trust officer to see how things are going," Shelby said. "Is this a nursing home or a prison?"

"It's a nursing home, with our own highly successful methods. We insist that our rules be followed. Reread your contract with us, Mr. Shelby." Dr. Cart stood for a moment, lost in thought. "*Write* your bank. That should be good therapy for you."

"Speaking of therapy, aren't there any trips outside?" Shelby asked. "I've got cabin fever." He couldn't admit he was lonely.

Cart shook his head. "We used to do trips, but we stopped. They were very traumatic for the patients. One man died on the bus and we had sheriffs and investigators all over us for days. It was very upsetting for us and the patients."

Shelby studied him. He remembered what Detmen had said. "Dite duck." And he remembered something else, something he'd read long ago in the newspapers about a doctor who'd specialized in quick-weight-loss diets, who'd given speed pills by the bucketful to his patients. Shelby remembered the scandal and the trial, but only vaguely. Had Cart's license been revoked?

"Before he died, Mr. Detmen said that you used to specialize in diet therapy, Dr. Cart. Is that true?"

Cart smiled coldly. "I came into the field of geriatrics some years ago when I decided to change my specialty." He examined Shelby with clinical eyes. "I'm reputed to be quite good in my new area of interest."

"I see," Shelby said. "But did you specialize in diets at one time?"

The doctor looked back at him without answering.

"I only asked," Shelby said softly . . .

For the first time Shelby had second thoughts about Eden. His fear of death had abated and what came to him in his first moments of suspicion was not renewed fear but anger. Could this place be some kind of trap for old people without close family or friends? Did they cage the unwary, get them to change their wills, then kill them with poor care or a pill? Or on an operating table, like tough old Detmen?

Thinking about it at length made the idea seem preposterous, but he continued to think about it anyway. Eden would be a perfect place to pull off such a scheme. What few visitors came would have little interest in the patients' concerns. Shelby knew better than most that the world was imperfect. He knew a hundred confidence schemes and how they were run.

He considered his situation. It would be profitless for them to kill him unless he changed his will in their favor. Then one day he saw Hoskins enter Kay's room and shut the door. Hearing him leave a short while later, he decided he would pay a visit to Kay himself that night.

He waited until late, until the night attendant had gone for coffee, and then entered the room next door. Kay's old eyes followed him from door to bed. Lost eyes.

"Do you remember me?" Shelby asked.

Nothing.

"I defended you once in court."

After a moment there was a tiny look of recognition. Kay nodded. "You defended me, devil."

When Kay said no more, Shelby opened the bedside table drawer. It was empty except for a sheaf of papers like those Shelby had received from Hoskins, legal papers concerning new wills and codicils to old ones. "Did you sign those papers for the home?"

"Today," Kay whispered. "I wanted it done." He turned his face away from Shelby and pulled the pillow closer to his head. "I killed her all those years ago," he said softly to the wall. "But the jury said I didn't kill her. You did that, devil."

"And now the staff here is going to let you die, is that it?" Shelby asked. "To reward you? Because you want that?"

Kay watched the wall without answering.

From far away there was a sound. Shelby left the room.

He was now fairly sure Eden was a murder trap, but there still seemed to be a reasonable doubt. He'd lived by reasonable doubt. Even if they let Kay die, that didn't make it certain they were killing others.

But there was enough evidence for Shelby to want out. There were other nursing homes. He sat on his bed and tried to figure a way of escaping Eden. He couldn't climb the fence or get out the guarded gate. Maybe he could hide in the backseat of a doctor's car. But he remembered seeing the guards looking in the backseats of departing cars. It had puzzled him until now. Then he had a thought. What about the letter Cart had suggested?

Shelby wrote a long, devious letter to his bank and delivered it to Dr. Cart. The letter asked that the bank send someone to the nursing home to see Shelby. He made the letter insistent and specified that they send a lawyer he'd known, making the lawyer seem to be a bank employee.

That was the day Kay died.

No one came to visit Shelby on the week that followed, or the one following that. One morning into the third week, while Shelby was preparing a new, more strident letter, something went wrong. Nausea and blackness. Dr. Cart was summoned quickly and Shelby's bed was pushed down the hall, through the staff door, and into an intensive-care room.

Shelby felt no pain, only a loss of seeing and being. He was hooked to monitoring devices. Dr. Cart gave him several injections and took his pulse and blood pressure. A nurse stood watch.

Inside Shelby's brain, when he could get around the drugs, he discovered anger.

If he lived—

He thought he might live. He could perceive them working feverishly, presumably toward that purpose.

He wandered away from consciousness.

Waking was difficult. It was hard to open his eyes, so he kept them closed.

There was no pain in his chest and his heartbeat seemed to be regular.

He could hear bits of conversation. He thought one voice was Dr. Cart's, soft but authoritative. He seemed to be in another room. "He does enough sedatives, that, doesn't solve our problems."

"Codicil—" That was Mr. Hoskins' unctuous voice.

"He won't do—" Yes, it was definitely Dr. Cart, but his words were difficult to make out.

"Who would hear? We can always give shock treatments if we have to."

"True. Perhaps we'll try. He'll be grateful we saved his life. But he's been a problem—always nosing around."

"He has money," Hoskins said firmly. "You know our kind of patient isn't easy to find."

Shelby's sick heart pounded alarmingly. There was no longer a reasonable doubt.

When he finally opened his eyes, a pretty nurse smiled at him with foxlike eyes. He remembered how to influence jurors and he smiled back.

"I'm alive," he said, as if amazed about it. "You've saved my life." His voice sounded shockingly weak.

The nurse smiled down at him and he reminded himself all of them were in on it. It couldn't work any other way. A whole staff of murderers. Forced bequests and sudden death for the contented, TV-addicted ancients, the good life for the staff.

Back in his room, he tried to get up, but his legs were gone. He was afraid of the food, but he ate it stoically. If it was drugged, there was no indication. He talked the nurse into bringing him a portable wheelchair.

He smiled at Cart and Hoskins and the rest of the staff. He was effusively grateful to them. He asked Hoskins for a new codicil form to study. He tried to appear weaker than he was and the eyes that had carefully watched him temporarily relaxed. He'd bought a little time.

When Hoskins visited again (with the codicil form), Shelby said: "I'll fill in a figure for you very soon. Give me a few days."

Two nights later he returned to the drug chest when the attendant was asleep. He opened both locks. A long life of cross-examining pathologists and lab technicians had made him aware of the power of some of the numbing and deadly things. Those with skull and crossbones in the chest he took on trust. Good enough for them, good enough for him.

A night attendant seeking clean linen almost caught him as he wheeled on toward the staff area, but he made it safely to the door and picked the lock with the manicure tool and a plastic credit card slipped down to hold open the lock. He rolled his chair inside and found the kitchen area.

He dumped only light sedatives into the steaming coffee

urn, trusting it would make the early coffee drinkers sleepy as they awaited the main course. He then used the poisons, tasting or smelling each additive gingerly and discarding any that were too bitter or too pungent. The pills he ground to a fine powder. Moving around slowly and with great care, he found a huge bowl of beaten eggs in the refrigerator and added a combination of the poisons. He put some of the poison in the freshly squeezed orange juice and more in the milk. There was a dispenser for mineral water at the end of a service table. There he was moderate, careful not to alter the color.

The staff would breakfast and then they would serve the late-rising patients. *If they could.*

A doctor might detect the poisons, but Shelby wondered if detection would be enough to save them all. Or many of them. He hoped not.

There would be sheriffs and state police, sirens and flashing lights. *Lovely.* Perhaps he'd be accused. Maybe he could conduct his own case. Cinch self-defense.

He rolled unseen back to his bed and napped for a time. Something in the drugs he'd tasted made his heart fibrillate wildly for a time, but it passed. He felt weak, but well enough when he got up a few hours later. When Mr. Hoskins came in the outside door, just before the staff breakfast hour, Shelby was there to meet him. He reached into a pocket of the chair cover and offered over the codicil.

"This is what I want," Shelby told the administrator. "If you'll bring two witnesses along sometime today I'll sign it." He started to turn away, then stopped. "Anytime after breakfast, but before *General Hospital.*"

Mr. Hoskins beamed when he read the figure Shelby had inserted.

"Have a good day," Shelby told him, moving off in the direction of his room.

On the Rocks

That was the late summer day later remembered at the club as the time five golfers went out for eighteen and only four came back after the first nine holes.

Sheriff Barger was one of the four survivors. He sat at a table in the bar with the other three.

"Now," he said, "I want to know exactly where everyone was when judge Hinshaw fell into the sharp rocks near the ninth hole?"

The ambulance had come and gone. It had entered the drive of the country club with red lights on and siren screaming, startling the children in the swimming pool, but it had left silently enough. *No need to hurry,* Barger thought.

"I lost my ball farther down the creek," Edwards, the newspaper editor, said. "It's not so steep down there and I saw it and went down for it." He sighed gustily. "I was hooking everything again. When the judge screamed I was trying to dig the ball out with a two iron and wishing I had some contraption like you carry, Sheriff, you know that telescoping thingamajig with a ball retriever on the end." He nodded. "All this and the triple bogie I took on the seventh hole have made me very nervous and thirsty. I'd like to have a drink. Can't we please have a drink now?"

Sheriff Barger relented. He didn't want them drunk and babbling, but he was thirsty himself. "Maybe one drink."

Edwards nodded up at Jan, the brown-eyed girl who usually tended bar stoically on Wednesdays and Saturdays when the Jug Finders played.

"I'll have a see-through screw, Jan." He smiled. He was a thin man, very devious, the poorest golfer in the group, but one who planned every shot to take maximum advantage of his failings. Because of the hook he drove off tees facing at about twenty degrees away from his hoped for line of flight.

"Make it a double since we're limited to one," Edwards added.

George Dart, the happy dentist, nodded. "Double that double order, Jan." He looked at Sheriff Barger. All the men at the table were in their fifties, sixties, or early seventies and they'd played golf together for a long time. The Jug Finders was a drinking society in addition to being a golfing group. On the course they fought each other for every dollar that went into the communal drinking pot, exultant about good holes, despondent about bad ones.

"How about you, Doc?"

"I was, as usual, in the woods. I'd sliced my second shot, also as usual. I didn't even hear the scream, but I'm getting a trifle hard of hearing."

That was true, Sheriff Barger thought. *Dart could occasionally hear a loud clap of thunder. But he had sharp eyes.*

"Did you see anything?"

"I came out and saw you all standing there and then saw Judge Hinshaw in the rocks." He looked at Barger. "Are you sure he was dead, Sheriff?"

"I'd stake my life on it," the fourth man said. He was a retired lawyer-banker who owned a chain of theaters. He was full of bright, sometimes dry remarks and he'd hated Judge Hinshaw enough to take a series of lessons from the pro to improve his game so as hopefully to beat the judge, Barger remembered. His name was Walter Rose.

"Where were you, Walter?" Barger asked.

Rose nodded at Jan to bring him another drink. He'd

evaded Barger's semiorder not to drink by getting a lemonade and then having Jan dump a double of gin into it. He'd claimed he needed it because of his "cough."

"I was in the cart. My second shot was over the creek. After I'd managed that with my trusty three wood I drove dutifully back and rang the bell so the group behind us could tee off. I think I may have heard the poor judge scream, but he'd been screaming and cheating for years and I didn't think much about it." He shrugged. "I didn't even bother to look."

Barger looked up at the pictures on the wall of the bar. There golfers clad in the clothes of their times stood proudly holding cups won for skill on the course. One could look long and far and discover few Jug Finders. They'd ritually be found in the bar bemoaning their luck when such winners' pictures were taken.

"As I recall," Sheriff Barger said to Rose, "you threatened the judge when we were playing the third hole."

"You know what he was doing?" Rose asked intently. "He hit his drive into the pines on the right. When I saw him, he was kicking it out into a good lie where he'd have an open second shot. Then he failed to count at least one shot he had on his adventurous way to the green. I saw him put down a five and he had a six at best."

"We should have made him quit keeping score long ago," Dr. Dart said. "He'd gotten into a new habit of subtracting a stroke from his score on a hole or two. Critical holes."

Edwards nodded. His fingertips were blue from printer's ink and Sheriff Barger thought he remembered seeing a smudge like that on Judge Hinshaw's yellow golf shirt.

"He was a genius with numbers, with misfiguring them, I mean. None of us ever understood how he figured things out and so we let him keep doing it and paid what he announced."

Jan picked that moment to bring the drinks. She handed Barger his lite and set the rest of the drinks on the table. Her voice was soft but firm. "I'll tell you another thing he was doing. He'd come in with you guys and take charge of the money and then he'd pocket some of it. He'd tell you he'd tipped me when he hadn't. All the time he'd be pinching me every time I got in range. I know you guys use all the money you lose to buy drinks, but it wasn't happening that way." She shook her head. "He was the cheapo to end all cheapos."

"Were you here in the clubhouse all afternoon?" Barger asked her.

"No, but I wasn't out on the course or one of you would have surely seen me." Jan gave them her best gamin smile. "I was doing what I was doing, but not with Judge Hinshaw. Dirty old man is what he was."

"All of us are that," Edwards admitted uncomfortably.

Jan smiled cryptically. "There are sexy senior golfers and there are dirty old men. I count you boys in the former group. I counted Judge Hinshaw in the latter." She shook her head firmly. "He made a pass at every woman who was dumb enough to get within 'gimme range.' "

"Makes me glad I'm single," Barger said.

"You're the only one who is. The rest of us and our wives have had to put up with his beastly ways for years," Rose said.

Sheriff Barger made his decision. "It has to have been an accident. If any of us had done it one of the others would have seen it. I was out of sight of him on top of the creek when he went in. Too bad it had to be at that one real bad spot where all the jagged rocks are. It sure tore him up."

"He stole golf balls, too," Dr. Dart mused. "On eight I'm certain he played my ball instead of his own. He wasn't that way when he started with us, was he?"

"Sort of," Edwards said. "He kept getting worse. Not only had his golf deteriorated, but my wife said he made a very firm pass at her the last time we went off on a golfing weekend."

"So did mine," Dr. Dart said, startled.

"Who's going to tell Mrs. Hinshaw?" Edwards asked.

"She knows," Jan said from behind the bar. "One of the other ladies came in from the course and said Ruth Hinshaw had gone to the funeral home to pick out a casket. She seemed to be taking it quite well. In fact she was described as being in good spirits."

"She should be," Dr. Dart said, sniffing. "He'd been giving her a hard way to go for the last twenty or thirty years." He nodded. "The one thing you can say about his golf game is that he was always very good out of sand traps."

Edwards shook his head. "If they were deep traps he'd yell 'fore' and then throw the ball up with a handful of sand."

"The prosecutor is going to ask questions," Sheriff Barger said, more in explanation than worry. "Even if Judge Hinshaw was retired there's a possibility the prosecutor will want to call the grand jury." He shook his head. "And multiple violations of the rules of golf wouldn't, more's the pity, be a defense to a murder charge if the prosecutor gets his back up."

"You leave that to me," Edwards said. "An accident is an accident. If the prosecutor starts wasting county money on something like this then I'm going to write a few editorials. And this is an election year."

"I'll talk to him also," the sheriff said. "Are we all agreed then? It was an accident? A tragic golfing accident?"

He had a chorus of nods. Even Jan, behind the bar, nodded.

"I suppose it would be unseemly to play the back nine?"

125

Rose said, his voice questioning. "I hate to lose the day. One can't count on days like this forever. Soon it'll be fall and then winter." He looked forlorn. "No golf."

"We could take a vote on it," Edwards said. "I'm for finishing the eighteen."

Rose nodded. Dr. Dart hesitated, then nodded also.

Sheriff Barger said, "To the tenth tee then." He watched them as they finished their drinks.

It had gone about as he expected it. Now all he needed to make certain of was that he'd not bent or jammed the telescoping ball retriever when he used it to topple Judge Hinshaw from the bank to the sharp rocks below.

They'd wait a suitable time and then he and Ruth Hinshaw could begin to openly see each other. He'd told her for several years she deserved more than the now deceased judge. And the culminating insult, Hinshaw's death warrant, had come on the sixth hole when Barger had caught Hinshaw trampling the green where Barger's putt must travel for a rare birdie attempt. Barger had missed the putt. There was cheating and there was *cheating*.

Sheriff Barger smiled at Jan and paid her for the drinks.

"It just goes to show," she said. "Cheaters never win."

Barger took his golf cap piously off and shook his head. "Let's not speak ill of the dead."

She leaned toward him, her voice a whisper. "In a few months, when this dies down, I'm going to make a special drink for you gentlemen. We'll call it privately 'Hinshaw on the rocks.' "

The Calculator

That was the year Cyril Ratchford abandoned practicing law until Hysell hired him for a dollar. It was a year that began badly, with Judge Evans granting a guardianship of the person on Ratchford. Ratchford felt no anger at Evans, who was an old friend. He even admitted during the judge's hearing that he had been drinking heavily since Connie had died, that his legs had recently given out, and that he'd not been eating properly—or hardly at all, for that matter.

Judge Evans appointed one of the young partners in Ratchford's law firm as guardian, and together they plotted and sent Ratchford to the Sunset Years Nursing Home. There he began to mend—or mend as much as can be expected of a seventy-year-old man with a bad liver and a problem heart.

Sunset Years was all right with Ratchford. The food was good and plentiful and his appetite returned. The attendants were friendly, although Ratchford quickly learned one didn't leave items worth stealing in view. His legs came back a little so that soon, with two stout canes and much effort, he could slowly get around.

The nursing home was full of old people and problem people, many of them forgotten or abandoned. Once Ratchford was well he soon got to know most of them and found they were people who'd lived uninteresting lives and were awaiting routine deaths. Ratchford, who'd spent his own life in deadly combat in courtrooms, found they mostly bored him.

There were minor exceptions. Down the hall there was a large old man who hit at people. He hit at attendants, nurses, doctors, and other patients—he was impartial about it. He liked to lie in wait and spring out from behind things, laughing and striking mean little blows.

The second time he did it to Ratchford, Ratchford thumped him with one of the canes. The large old man cried a little and seemed confused and hurt about it, and refused to lie in wait for Ratchford thereafter.

There was also a lady who had something growing inside her head and could no longer communicate. She talked but none of the words associated or made sense. Now and then she would stumble into Ratchford's room, fall into the lone chair, and blather away, very bewildered and earnest about it.

Ratchford found himself, more and more as time wound down for him, enmeshed in a vague ennui. He resisted attempts to get him back to the office. When he was asked if he wanted to move elsewhere he recoiled from the idea. Sunset Years was home.

He did have his guardian instruct the nursing home management that he should be allowed to wander outside by himself.

Outside was where he re-met John Hysell.

Sunset Years had once been a resort hotel-motel until cooler winters and newer motels had forced it into receivership. It had then been picked up by the nursing home chain which now operated it. Ratchford thought his firm might have handled some of the transactions.

Across the road from the rambling main nursing home building he found a path that led down between huge beach houses to the sea. Partway down the path, leading from the largest mansion—now in disrepair and seemingly aban-

128

doned—someone had built a new boardwalk continuing to the beach and terminating in a roofed lookout complete with a weathered picnic table. The lookout was open from floor to roof, but the breeze was pleasant there and the roof kept the sun from being too fierce.

So during the days, to escape the talker and to avoid the accusing eyes of the bully man, Ratchford would take a book and walk laboriously to the lookout. Sometimes he'd read, other times he sat watching the birds and the waves and the passing boats, sharing the luck of occasional fishermen and observing the beach walkers who passed.

The third time he was there John Hysell came. He came from the huge, half-ruined house, and Ratchford didn't know him at first. He rode in an electric wheelchair fabricated of shiny aluminum, and he operated it smartly. He wheeled into the lookout and smiled at Ratchford. He was carrying an ornate box on his blanket-covered lap. In one shirt pocket Ratchford spied a thin battery-powered calculator.

"You play checkers?" he asked.

Ratchford saw that Hysell's legs were useless under the thin lap blanket. His left arm was also affected. But the right arm still worked some and, above the neck, he seemed all right—smiling and waiting for an answer.

"I play checkers, chess, cribbage, gin rummy, and anything else you can think of." Connie had been a game fanatic.

Hysell's face tilted. "Don't I know you?"

"Cyril Ratchford. I am—or was—a lawyer."

Hysell nodded. "You did some work for me years back. And I built you a house. I'm John Hysell."

Ratchford remembered. Hysell had been a young, intent engineer-builder. Ratchford had later heard Hysell had made a fortune in construction and acquired a reputation as a man who did things right. He had built Connie's dream house when Ratchford could barely afford dreams, and it had continued to be her dream house until she died. In Florida, where anything built could be sold, Ratchford had been grateful.

"I've been watching you from what the last hurricane left of the balcony," Hysell said, pointing up. "I like the way you swing down here on those canes—like it was an effort but worth it. I'm not allowed out by my sweet new wife, Miss Two-Ton, but today she went to a bingo party and by now she's probably stuffed herself full of ice cream and cake. It was easy to sneak past the maid. She takes a nap every time Miss T-T goes out."

"Your wife doesn't understand you," Ratchford said, smiling.

"Very perceptive," Hysell said, smiling in return. He appraised Ratchford—the expensive clothes, the white hair. "She'd like *you*," he said.

"Is that good?"

"No, not really," Hysell said. "She has a history of not picking her males for permanence." He thought for a minute, looking away so that Ratchford could no longer see his face. "Can I hire you?"

"Perhaps. I'm still a lawyer, although I've been inactive."

Hysell found a worn dollar in one of his pockets. He handed it up. "Consider yourself retained."

"For what?"

"What I really need is someone to help me kill my wife. Would you do that? No?" He shook his head. "I shouldn't have asked. I can read the shock in your eyes."

"I'm only a lawyer," Ratchford said. He looked down at the troubled man. "I can be hired only for that kind of work." He hesitated and then put the dollar in his pocket. "Have been hired," he amended.

Hysell sighed. "I've never really understood your profession. I suppose that now if anything happened to her you'd report me, wouldn't you?"

"No, I wouldn't. Some lawyers would. It's a technical point of ethics. I'm going to treat what you told me as a privileged communication."

Hysell nodded. "Well, if you won't help and you won't tell, that puts us back into the checkers area." He handed over the lap box. Ratchford opened it and found an exquisite folding checkerboard.

"The checkers are in that little drawer. We turn them over for kings." He smiled. "I shouldn't stay too long. Next time I'll sneak away as soon as she goes. But she doesn't go often. She's the meanest, most calculating woman I've ever known. My third wife." He lost the smile.

"I see."

"I remember when we were younger you did a lot of criminal work, Mr. Ratchford. Did you ever defend anyone accused of killing his wife?"

Ratchford nodded. "Many times."

Hysell shook his head. "It's such a problem. She's big and strong. I bumped her once accidentally with my chair and she stopped me cold. I put some stuff in her wine, some corrosive cleaner, but she spit it out. She watches me all the time so I can't go out and buy a gun." He shook his head. "I used to be a good engineer. Now I can't do anything but operate this infernal chair and play with my calculator. It lowers the possibilities. So I suppose she'll just sit and wait for me to die." He shook his head. "She won't even let me live someplace decent." He looked up at the old wind-damaged house. "She inherited that from her last husband."

"Divorce her," Ratchford said.

"She told me if I try to divorce her she'll hold it up and

maybe get me committed. Probably to a place like your Sunset Years. Could she do that?"

"Perhaps." Ratchford considered the ruined man before him. "Maybe even probably." He remembered the frustrating years in practice, the slowness, the frequent futility. "Getting a divorce can take a while, but Sunset Years is all right."

"I wouldn't mind that much, but I don't want her to realize it. Not too long ago some policemen came looking for her and questioned her about one of her husbands who died. I think she knows she has to treat me carefully." He looked out at the sea, a long look. "When we were married she talked me into putting a lot of things into joint title. When I die my two kids will get next to nothing.

"She put on almost a hundred pounds after I had my stroke. She can let me die, but I think right now she's afraid to do more. So she'll outwait me, if she doesn't eat herself to death. She went on a diet when I first met her. That was when I imagined she loved me. Now she picks and punishes and argues, trying to hasten me along. And she eats and eats." He shook his head, sick and bewildered. "How did a smart engineer wind up in a mess like this?"

"Why not make her mad enough to put you in Sunset Years?"

Hysell nodded and smiled craftily. "I'll bet that's where she'd put me. She's too smart to let me get far out of sight, too fat and lazy to want to travel far to see me dying. Sunset Years would be convenient." He gave Ratchford an odd, calculating look. "She'd see you there too. While she's involved in that maybe I could . . ."

All of it meant nothing to Ratchford, but Hysell had been a joy to Connie in building her house. He owed him semi-free advice and counsel for that.

"You can try," he said.

A few days later Ratchford found Hysell as the newest resident of Sunset Years, ensconced in a double room with a man named Schmidt who continually muttered terrible things about his family. Ratchford had thought Schmidt pitiful and had avoided the man's room. Schmidt's family were all dead.

Hysell smiled up at him from a bed. "She took my wheelchair away when we first started arguing, but I'll get it back. She's got some tax papers I have to sign and she's afraid to forge my signature." He nodded. "Look in my nightstand drawer."

Ratchford did. Inside was a deck of plastic playing cards and a fancy cribbage board.

"You're better at checkers than I am, but I'm going to beat you to death playing cribbage," Hysell announced. He punched some numbers on the ever-present calculator. "The odds are two to one."

They were playing that afternoon when Mella Hysell came visiting.

"Who are you?" she asked Ratchford from the door. Her face was all arched eyebrows and full cheeks, but Ratchford could see she was a handsome woman. Even far overweight she'd never be ugly—blimpish, but very pretty. She looked thirty years younger than Hysell.

Ratchford stood up haltingly. She watched him with eyes that seemed sympathetic.

"My name's Cyril Ratchford. Your husband was instructing me in a game called cribbage." He smiled at her. He'd been charming juries all his life.

"And you live here?" she asked, smiling back.

"Temporarily," Ratchford said.

She fussed around Hysell's bed, fluffing the pillows, straightening the sheets, all the time watching Ratchford.

"I brought those papers," she told Hysell in a low, intent voice. "Sign them now and I'll bring over your wheelchair."

"Bring my chair and *then* I'll sign," Hysell answered.

She nodded, still watching Ratchford, who was beginning to feel like a snake being eyed by a mongoose. "I started my diet today," she said to both men.

Hysell laughed. "I'll bet."

She gave him a baleful look. "Well, I did. And you know when I make my mind up to it I can do anything." She calculated him and the room. "Be nice and I'll bring you home."

"It's more restful here," Hysell demurred. "Or it will be when I get my chair."

"You'll get your chair when you come home."

Hysell smiled. "I'll sign the papers then too."

She smiled. "Whatever will Mr. Ratchford think of us—quarreling in front of him." She nodded at Ratchford. "He argues with me sometimes, but he knows what Momma says is best."

Ratchford smiled politely.

After she'd gone, Hysell seemed unwilling to go back to the cribbage game. He was pensive.

"Cyril," he said, "you must know some criminals. Couldn't you contact someone for me to hire? I know I can't last a lot longer."

Ratchford shook his head. "Let's suppose I did. If you made a deal, in law, I could be as guilty as you. Besides, your wife doesn't seem so bad. I think you're exaggerating."

Hysell gave him a penetrating glance. "She was interested in you, just as I predicted. By the time she sees you again she'll have checked you out. She took one look at your white

134

hair and decided she was going to lose weight." He nodded. "She did that for me too. She was married then, to a man with a bad heart. He died shortly after I met her."

"You keep saying things like that. You talk about police and such. Are you saying she killed her last husband?"

"All I'm telling you are my suspicions. When we were married, for example, she admitted to two previous marriages. From what she's let slip and from what I've deduced since then, I've got to be at least number five or six. Those earlier husbands had to pass out of the picture somehow." He shook his head. "She's a creature for our time, Cyril. Florida abounds with old people. Mella's especially apt at caging the males of the species. She becomes impatient when she's not hunting. So I must watch myself and plan." He smiled. "One thing's for sure—she'll lose weight now."

"Many people diet."

Hysell shook his head. "Mella loves to eat. She'll lose now for one reason only. She means to impress you."

"I quite probably don't have as much time left on this earth as you do," Ratchford protested.

"She wouldn't be interested in you if you had a lot of time left," Hysell replied. "I wish you'd help me. Just a name and a telephone number would do for starts."

"I'm a lawyer, not an assassin."

"Fair enough. I'll just ask for one thing then—one favor. Show some interest in her."

Ratchford hesitated, then nodded, intrigued.

Ratchford found Mella Hysell the most direct and forward woman he'd ever known. It was as if she knew she could say whatever she wanted and that he was too much of a gentleman to argue or disagree.

Like the hitting man, she lay in wait for him, stalking him.

Hysell took to sleeping away the long afternoons. That meant Ratchford must either spend the afternoons in his own room, lost in the agonies of daytime television, or go outside and cripple his way to the lookout area.

When he knew she waited for him he tried to find another alternative, but he was unsuccessful. Other than the path to the sea there was little of interest, and there was no other way to get to the beach within reasonable distance. To the north there were scores of tiny tract houses, most of them occupied by pensioners from the North. To the south there were more large homes, most of them damaged and unoccupied, then a bait store, then a boat place. Neither was a place to spend the long afternoons, although he tried, wandering north, then south.

So he went back to the lookout.

She waited for him on the unrailed balcony. At first she wore long concealing dresses. Later, as her weight diminished, she went to daring things—no bra, and finally bikinis.

Ratchford was alarmed, flattered, intrigued, and half a dozen other things all at once. She was perceptive to this, playing on his moods like a skilled harpist. If he seemed alarmed at the speed or direction of the ersatz affair, she soothed him. If he asked about her past life, she lied well. If he foresaw a dismal future, she always pictured them together in it.

"John isn't well," she told him. "He hates me because of that. He can't last much longer, his doctors say. And I need someone, Cyril. Someone like you—experienced, urbane." She'd accompany these speeches with a melting look that became more and more effective as her excess flesh vanished. Ratchford estimated her weight loss after eight weeks at almost forty pounds. It went more slowly thereafter, but she continued to lose. It was as if, knowing the strength of her web, she knew it would support only a lean spider.

Hysell watched and, after a while, laughed at Ratchford, but it was a laugh which understood and sympathized.

"Now you know," he said.

Ratchford shook his head, not knowing.

"In your practice how many divorces did you obtain for women?"

"Hundreds, perhaps thousands," Ratchford said.

"Didn't any of those women try to latch onto you?"

Ratchford nodded. Some had, and it had been an agony for him to treat them nicely. Connie was alive then and she was the only woman for him. There had been divorcees who clutched and cried and promised multitudes of delights. Some had been beautiful. All had been interested in matrimony, a replacement of the one shed in court. But none of them, not even the best schemer he remembered, had been as good at intrigue as Mella Hysell. He found himself enjoying the performance, and uncertain as to whether he was moved by it or not.

There was a sane Ratchford who stood in the shadows watching all.

What would you do with her? the sane Ratchford asked. *I mean, what good would she be to you?*

But he could dream and he was intrigued. It was as if, in what he knew to be the last of life, he was to be allowed once again to engage in a "first affair."

"How much weight do you figure she's lost by now?" Hysell constantly asked, using his good hand to doodle on his calculator. "Does she still wait for you on the balcony?"

"She's your wife," Ratchford told him. "This is embarrassing me. I think you should come with me."

Hysell shook his head. "She has my chair. She's using it to

get me to come home, and I think it'll be time soon." He doodled some more with the calculator, cleared it, and snapped it off. "Not quite yet though. Tell me what you see in her."

Ratchford shook his head. "She's young. She's ardent. She has definite ideas about things. And she's vivid and handsome. Sometimes I feel as if I'm in distress and she's a knight riding to my rescue. She reverses the roles of romance."

Hysell smiled. "Those were my feelings exactly."

"But not now?" Ratchford said.

"Mella is interested mainly in the chase and the capture, not the afterwards. She'll pursue you as she chased me. Sooner or later you'll become the pursuer. Then she will temporize, demand plans, ask various conditions to prove your love. When you accede she'll marry you." He smiled. "By that time I'll be dead and you'll be the heir apparent."

Ratchford, realizing that Mella had already forced things between them close to the temporizing stage, said nothing.

"I tell her I hate you when I see her alone," Hysell confided. "She tells me to come home and look after my business. She understands jealousy." He smiled. "I'm not jealous. I'm only trying to figure some neat way to do her in before she does me in, but ideas that seem workable are hard to come up with. For her it would be easy. Too much or too little medicine, perhaps a pillow over the face or a fall down the steps—" He smiled again, more interested than afraid. "She's a lot stronger than either of us, Cyril. With your help, I might kill her more easily." He gave Ratchford an inquiring look.

Ratchford shook his head.

"Remember, when I go you'll be next."

"What if I'm not interested in her?"

"But you are," Hysell explained.

★ ★ ★ ★ ★

A few days later Hysell was gone. A nurse told Ratchford that Mella had taken him home. Ratchford waited for him at the lookout, but only Mella came.

"Where's John?" he asked, careful not to show too much interest.

"He's not feeling well," she said quickly. "He's failing, I'm afraid. Soon to be with me no more." She shook her head and Ratchford was unsurprised at the tears in her eyes. "Then I'll be alone."

He waited.

"It's been the story of my life. I've fallen in love with mature men. First John, then you. Now John will die and leave me." She eyed him warmly.

Ratchford, fascinated but wary, had a problem holding himself back from offering the wanted substitute.

"I'd like to see John," he said.

She inclined her head. "I know he's told you stories. I hope you don't believe them. I'll bring him out onto the balcony tomorrow so you can see him." The tears became profuse, and it was hard to disbelieve them. "It may be for the last time."

She groped for his hand and held it.

The next day he went early to the lookout and waited. After a time he was rewarded. John and Mella came onto the balcony. They waved to him, Mella enthusiastically, John feebly. Ratchford hobbled up the boardwalk to be closer, to call out to them.

Suddenly, without Ratchford seeing why, Mella flew down, screaming, to join him, her black-and-white-print dress fluttering in the sea breeze as she fell. By the time he got to her she was dead, her eyes unseeing, her now thin body lying broken on the flagstones.

After a while John appeared on the boardwalk. He rolled down to Ratchford in his aluminum chair.

"She stopped my medicine," he said. "I think she was sure that would do it. I acted as if it was about to, but I feel all right." He looked down at her and did one more calculation on his calculator. "She'd lost a lot of weight. Just enough."

Ratchford nodded. "Have you ever told anyone else the things you told me?"

"Regrettably, yes."

"Well, tell no one else. And somehow you've picked up a bit of black-and-white cloth on the front of the arm to your chair."

Hysell nodded, his color better than Ratchford had ever seen it.

"Are you sure you're all right?" Ratchford asked.

"I'm fine."

"Certainly there's no way you could feel well enough to talk with the police about this tragic fall. When they arrive, you'll answer no questions. After all, your wife is dead." He looked at Hysell, whose good right hand was working at the nooks and crannies of the arm of his chair.

"Every thread," Ratchford ordered.

Savant

Dr. Morgan sat with his back to the office window and listened.

"The sheriff's out here again today," Mrs. Lord, the hospital administrator, said severely.

"I saw him around my building."

"They did the autopsy. He's seen the preliminary findings and he's not satisfied with them." Mrs. Lord looked out her window imperiously. "I'm not, either. A child just doesn't die without reason, even a child as profoundly retarded as Sandra."

"I'm puzzled about it also, but I'm afraid I can't add anything," Morgan said. He looked at his watch. It was time to be back on the ward that was the focal point of his life these days.

She looked critically down at a file that he presumed to be his and then over his head and out her window, surveying her domain. He knew she liked everything tidy, and he had no objection to its being that way as long as her orderliness didn't interfere in his life.

"Outside" was a state mental hospital, a gathering of ramshackle buildings, recreation areas, and farmland. Once it had been all retarded children, but a falling state budget had combined the children with adults. Tax money for the retarded and the mentally ill existed at the far edges of a politician's dream.

"Your appointment as a permanent staff member comes up next month. What am I supposed to tell the board then?"

He shook his head cynically, not knowing, not particularly caring. A fourteen-year-old girl with a life history of profound mental retardation following postnatal cerebral infection had died. Most like that in his ward were forgotten, abandoned by their parents, unvisited and unwanted. But Sandra was one of the rare ones whose family still visited frequently, a family living close by the hospital. They'd gone to the prosecutor and sheriff. Investigators now prowled the halls of his wards, where the most profoundly retarded were, asking the attendants questions, making notes. The newspapers had gotten into the death recently. Their stories had been vague but suspicious.

"Nothing else unusual on your ward?" she asked carefully. Her degrees were in business, not medicine, and he and Mrs. Lord shared no common purpose. She was an administrator, he was a doctor.

"There's never anything usual on it. Children change. Even children who are profoundly retarded learn small, new things, develop new symptoms." He almost reminded her about Kelly but decided not to. Kelly was the one person on the ward whom investigators could talk to if Kelly wanted to talk. But Kelly was delicate and had her own problems. She was blind, retaining only the ability to tell light from shadow, and her days and strength were spent in eagerly sculpting the heads she remembered from when she'd had sight, or new ones she felt with her inquiring fingers.

A savant. Idiot savant. The sculpted heads were beautifully done, and Morgan had written to Kelly's family about them more than a year back—with no reply and now none expected. Kelly was twenty-six years old. Until a few years back, she'd been able to see but had not interacted well with her peers or the staff, nor had the gift. Morgan had read the reports. Loss of vision from glaucoma had sent her on a strange inward journey. When Morgan had come to the hospital, Kelly had not communicated. Now she talked, but only when she wanted to talk. The heads were her obsession.

Mrs. Lord went on for more minutes. Morgan, listening to her, found that he cared nothing about whether or not he was reappointed. There were other hospitals, and hospitals like this were so understaffed with doctors trained also as psychiatrists that even scandal wasn't likely to keep him from finding a new job. He was used to scandal. He knew he had drinking and drug problems. Mrs. Lord knew it also and had known it when he was hired. He thought she was examining him covertly today to see what shape he was in.

Not too bad, lady. I'm trying to cut back. Maybe one day I'll quit.

He escaped to the wards. Once there he took a strong pill to catch up. For a while he read the paper, but the news was, as usual, bad. Someone had assassinated another leader in India. Terrorists had commandeered a jetliner in Italy. The Soviets claimed they had new weapons, and new defenses against old weapons. The national debt was growing alarmingly.

Somehow the whole system had gone wrong and was so ponderous that no one could now change it. He put the paper into the wastebasket. The hate that still smoldered within him was reserved mostly for the system and those who kept it painfully going, fighting about money for weapons and money for hunger, wasting two units for every unit spent usefully, internationally preying savagely on each other. One day soon they'd have to use all those weapons, if only for the sake of economy, and blow the planet up.

The thought was not unsatisfying.

His wards were painted in calm colors. Children and adults lay in ugly wooden orthopedic carts, many of them home-crafted in the shops of the state hospital. The patients stared up at the ceiling, most of them seeing nothing, non-verbal and nonambulatory. Sandra had been like that. And then, without symptom or warning, she'd died.

He read the charts and visited the two wards he had primary responsibility for. He prescribed Dilantin, Phenobarbital, Mellaril, Thorazine, and Valium for spasticity and seizures. He prescribed for constipation, incipient bedsores, and aggressive behavior. When he was exhausted and done, he illegally prescribed some Dilaudid for himself.

With that accomplished, he escaped to Kelly.

Kelly lay in her own cart. She was a thin, small woman with already graying hair. Her face was remote and unpretty. Morgan thought she was aware of what went on around her, that she heard everything. How much she understood of what she heard was questionable. He'd tried to give her the various intelligence tests available, but she'd been uninterested. He assessed her as brilliant in the area of her savant power, dull to normal in all others.

Today Kelly was talkative.

"Man came in. Asked about girl who died. Wanted to know what I knew." She shook her head, upset somehow by the questioning.

Morgan waited. When Kelly stopped, Morgan prompted her, "What do you know, Kelly? What did you tell the man?"

"Made her head once. Her mother came and saw what I do. Brought Sandra close, and I touched and then made a face out of the clay." She looked up at the bright window that lay above her. "Can see her like she was. She was sick."

"How sick?" Morgan asked, interested.

Kelly answered as she usually did when her interest waned. "I don't know. You want me to make your head now?"

"Sometime. Soon now." He liked this child-woman, but the thought of her fingers on his face was repugnant to him. He no longer wanted to be close to any person.

At times he daydreamed that he was terminally ill and heavily armed, ready to take his own revenge on an uncaring world. It was something that could take his mind away from worse memories.

"I make heads, and Nurse Datal bakes so they last," Kelly said, happy about it.

"I know," Morgan said. "Why do you make the heads, Kelly?" He was feeling pretty good now, floating a little, all pain and remembrance dim. The wife and daughter who'd vanished in the flames no longer insistently called to him. He could forget them.

"See them inside my head." Kelly nodded, still happy. "Have to make them. Once I could see many things, but now what I see is inside my head."

Conversation waned. Morgan liked Kelly and sensed Kelly also liked him. It was enough to sit close to the cart, to be there, to make Kelly a tiny part of the thing he'd lost, an ersatz substitute.

For a time Morgan slept in the chair by Kelly's cart. He was awakened by a hand on his shoulder.

"I need to talk with you again, Dr. Morgan," Sheriff Boonburger ordered heavily. "So wake up."

Morgan nodded and got up. He led the sheriff to his office. He found in the walk there that he was trembly, and his watch told him it was past time for something, maybe some Demerol. His taste in drugs had become more catholic down the years.

Morgan took a chair, and the sheriff towered above him—squeaking leather belt, boots, and gun—making Morgan nervous, making him want to reach out and grab the gun and fire it until it was empty.

"I'm wondering if you got any new ideas on why the girl died?"

Morgan shook his head.

"You have charge of the ward. You give the pills out, prescribe for the patients here. The results of the drug tests on Sandra haven't come back yet, but the thought now is that she may have died from an overdose of something. What were you giving her?"

Morgan tried to remember. Except for Kelly, somehow the ward residents all seemed to fall into one mass of gasping, cruel mouths, sick and angry screams, dumb silence, and violent seizures. He reached for Sandra's chart. "She got Valium for spasticity and Phenobarbital for seizures. She got some suppositories to ease elimination." He smiled without humor. "At the time she died, her worst medical situation appeared to be that she had hemorrhoids."

"How often did she have seizures?"

Morgan shrugged. "Sometimes she'd get two in one day. Sometimes, when we had her well controlled, she'd not get one for a month or two. She'd been in good shape for a month."

"Did she have some kind of seizure when she died?"

"You know she didn't, Sheriff."

The sheriff looked at him. "You don't volunteer a lot of information, do you, Doctor?"

"What do you want the information for?"

"To find out what happened."

"People have died here before. I'm sure you know that. These people lie for years in orthopedic carts, they're fed diet foods, they get no exercise except what the physical therapists give them. Most of them can't even tell us when something goes wrong. They tend to have strokes, heart problems. They seem to develop cancer more easily and more often than normal people." Morgan shook his head. "You weren't interested in the other deaths we've had here. Why the interest in this one?"

"Their fathers weren't on my county council," the sheriff said. "He don't like what happened, and therefore I don't like it, either. And when I checked on you, I didn't like what I got told, Doctor."

Morgan waited, feeling a chill run through him.

"One place we called said you were a practicing lush and a doper, that you'd had some accident tragedy in your family and it turned you into something with a bad smell to it. Some other places you've been were very evasive. I'm now wondering, if we don't find a cause for Sandra's death, if her old man would let us all off the hook and give up his crusade if you just packed on out of here—resigned?"

"Is that what you want?" Morgan asked. "Would that satisfy you and your local politicians?"

"Maybe, but not until all the results are in from the lab tests. Then we'll see what will satisfy my people."

Morgan found he was having trouble concentrating. He felt hot inside and he hurt all over. He needed something soon—codeine, Percodan, Darvon, Demerol. Something.

The sheriff moved to the door. "You wait," he warned. "Don't try to leave."

When the sound of footsteps had receded completely away, Morgan took another pill. He got a bottle out of the bottom drawer of his desk and had a long pull of vodka to wash the narcotic down.

Waking was the hardest thing. In sleep there was refuge because there were seldom dreams. But when he awoke, all the dreams that had gathered on the horizon and been unable to get through the wall of drugs and alcohol he had erected awaited him again. Awakening in the office was always to the odors of the hospital. The stench was a mixture of rot, urine, and coffee this morning.

He lay on the couch in his office. He remembered the accident, being thrown clear. He'd tried to walk, then finally to crawl to the burning car, but he'd been unable. All he could do was listen to the screams that came from the flames. Wife and six-year-old daughter. Beautiful daughter. Not like Kelly. Not ugly and blind.

The other driver had been drunk, had been driving his old uninsured clunker at high speed on the wrong side of the road with a suspended license. Nothing much had happened to him. A slap on the wrist. Six months, suspended.

Morgan had been sober and drug-free. But not afterward.

Others said it would only take time and he'd forget, but he'd not forgotten, and now it was five years.

Physician, heal thyself. He'd tried, but found no cure. And now he was as he was, competent enough when he wasn't too strung out on drugs or alcohol, but unable to hold a job for very long because of his almost visible habits. A year or two one place, six months at another. A hobo doctor, embittered, puzzling to his peers, and perpetually angry.

He got up and found black coffee. He examined his face in the mirror of his office. He noted without interest that he was thinner than he'd been, and wondered when he'd last eaten a real meal. He saw that his eyes seemed almost transparent. He took a pill. A pill or a drink was his cure for everything. He could rail at himself because it was that way, but he could no longer change it. He'd even turned himself in once, been on an addiction ward for sixty days, then gone immediately back to the drugs when released. After a binge.

He was, he decided, like the world around him, gravely

ill, terminal. No hope.

He went out into the wards and managed the morning routine. Nothing untoward seemed to have happened. Those who wet the bed had wet the bed. Those who could feed themselves were now doing it with varying degrees of success. Attendants fed the others. Many of the patients were on special diets. The attendants he passed eyed him curiously, and he wondered what the stories about him were now. His interest in them was minor, but curiosity remained.

He knew that once, a long time back, five years now, he'd been a good doctor. He knew that now he no longer was. He hadn't read anything in those five years, and his interest in psychiatry and medicine continued only because it gave him access to the drugs he needed to survive a while longer. His only fascination was in his own bitterness and feeding it, in dreaming of the world's damnation.

At two the sheriff came. He motioned Morgan to his office. Morgan followed the bigger man. Sheriff Boonburger took his chair, so Morgan sat meekly in the other one.

"They've called a grand jury, Doc." The sheriff watched him curiously, perhaps seeking some reaction. Morgan felt pretty good, about right. He smiled and nodded.

"I think probably they'll indict you for involuntary manslaughter real quick," the sheriff said, relishing his bombshell, still watching.

"Why would they do that?"

"Maybe because this year's election year. The girl died. She was in your care. You got drug problems. So you'll get indicted. Sometime tonight or tomorrow. I'll come out for you then. They're going to ask for a big bond. That means you'll be boarding with me." He watched Morgan with snow-cold eyes. "When I put you in, I'm going to strip search you. You won't have any pills to help you, no bottle of booze to hide behind. I figure you'll break wide open in maybe two or three days. You'll tell me anything I want to hear just because I want to hear it."

"But you know I wasn't even close to that girl when she died, and you have no evidence that I either failed to do something for her or did something to her that caused her death."

"She's dead, Doc. She was your patient. I can smell your breath from here. I can read your eyes. I've seen guys like you a hundred times. I'm not fooled. You'll break for me."

"I see," Morgan said, not seeing, but realizing the finality of it.

He planned. He figured out what was available and what it would require. Enough of these and he'd go to sleep and not wake up, enough of those and he'd float off and drown in his own juices.

No one to say goodbye to. Maybe Kelly. He chose the drowners.

He took a massive dose and wandered out into the ward. By the time he got to Kelly, it was hard to see, hard to navigate. Death was a soon-to-be thing.

He took Kelly's hand and woke her up from sleep.

"I came to say goodbye," he said. He noticed clinically that his voice wasn't slurred yet, but that the rest of him felt that way.

"Where do you go?" The sightless eyes sought him without success. "Why do you go?"

"It's time for me to go. I need to be with my family."

"Bring your head close. Let me touch your face. I want to sculpt you before you leave. I am sorry you leave." Tears came in her eyes. She shook her head. "I need you here. It's so lonely."

It seemed a small favor with death coming on. Morgan lowered his head and felt the small, inquiring fingers touch here and there, delicate as flowers, soft and smelling faintly of clay and urine. Something more than that came. There was a feeling of small, unexpected pain. There was momentary sickness and a small wrenching as if part of his head had been parted from the rest. He did not, in that moment, forget wife and daughter, but in a way, from that time on, he no longer remembered them in the same way.

It was the drug. He knew it was the drug.

When he found himself again, he felt rested and relaxed. He saw that Kelly was using the clay by the bed, the ever-present clay, clever hands already busily working. The head began to take shape.

Morgan was tired. He decided there was no time left to watch.

Morgan went back to his office. The deep pit he'd sought came, and he fell into it.

But it ended.

He came awake when he heard attendants moving about in the ward. He came up from sleep refreshed. He went for coffee and ate a roll. He went back to his office and got out a pill. He didn't feel he needed it, but the old habits were strong. The sheriff would be along sometime, and he wanted to be fortified for that. If death wasn't to be, then the last of life here would be pleasant. He wondered why death had not come. He was puzzled by it, but had no regret. He'd tried. Maybe he'd built up too much tolerance, and no drug could kill him? It seemed possible, if improbable.

The pill tasted bitter. Bile rose within him, and he found he must spit it out, not swallow it.

Outside, through the window, he saw a sheriff's car arrive.

He went to Kelly's cart. She lay there serene and unseeing,

but knowing he was there. Waiting.

"You did something," he said to her in a low voice.

She looked at him with sightless eyes. She smiled slightly. "At first I only made the heads. Now I can do things inside some of them. I don't know how. I only know that when I touch someone, I can do this. I tried with Sandra a week before she died, when her mother came here. There was something bright deep there, but the walls were too high when I tried to reach in. Then it got all black inside. I could see she was going to die. I touched other things, but the blackness stayed." Tears came in her eyes. "It made me feel bad that she died, but I didn't know what to do about it."

"You didn't want her to die," he said soothingly.

She nodded. "No. I wanted her to live. I'm learning. Every day I try to learn. With these in here, there's nothing more to learn. They are dark inside and empty, like Sandra." She nodded up at him. "Once before, I reached up inside and touched blackness like Sandra's. I did it on purpose. He died also."

"Oh? Who was that?"

"Dr. Street. He touched me, he touched others, where he shouldn't have touched us. He was sick inside, all light and dark mixed, so I touched him as he was touching me. I touched until it turned dark red. When I see inside a head like that, I have to do something." She smiled, not sorry. "Sometimes I can change them. I changed you. I saw you were sick and unhappy, and I changed you." Her voice held a note of triumph.

He remembered Dr. Street. The man had owned a reputation for sexual bizarreness. He'd died suddenly a year back, been found dead in his room. The autopsy had said aneurysm.

"What exactly do you do inside a head?" he asked, chilled

at the idea of it, but not that upset that people had died. Death was a part of life, of his life. That she could cause it intrigued more than frightened him.

She looked up at him with blind eyes. "It's like the other thing I do, the thing of making heads. I don't know. I only know what to do when I get there. I don't know how or why. And I also know I must do it. Even after Sandra and Dr. Street. Something inside my own head says I must do it."

"Yes," Morgan said. "Yes, I believe that." He leaned close. The sheriff had entered the ward. "Would you like for me to come back for you, to take you away from here, to take you places where you can sculpt many heads, heads full of light, perhaps even a few full of light and dark, like Dr. Street?"

"Yes. Oh, yes." She smiled at the sun-filled window. It was the first time he'd seen her truly excited.

"Wait, then. Tell no one else what you've told me. Wait for me."

Morgan spent long days in jail. Inside he ate as he'd not eaten in five years. He painted doors and walls for the sheriff. He talked learnedly when asked questions by the sheriff and deputies, trying to make them like him, trying to be of use.

One night, when a drunk went berserk, he helped quell him. He was pleasant and cooperative. He knew nothing about Sandra's death. The lab reports showed nothing new. Sandra was just dead.

Morgan said nothing about Kelly.

Newspaper reporters came and talked with him. He was pleasant to them, repeating the same story to them that he'd told the sheriff. He could see the sheriff watching him, then smiling at him. Attitudes shifted. The sheriff came past his cell and talked to him about signing a paper promising not to sue anyone. Morgan readily agreed.

He spent the time planning and thinking. He knew almost nothing about idiot savants, but knew he would read and find out more soon. He only knew, from books he'd read long before, that they existed; that there were those who could listen to music and play it back; others who could tell you what day of the week any date, past or present, occurred; others who could remember or add or multiply numbers. A gift to replace what retardation had taken?

Perhaps Kelly had the final gift, the gift perhaps for the times. He found that exciting, a new and better thing to daydream on. He no longer wanted revenge. Perhaps that had gone at the same time the drug addiction vanished. Now he wanted change. And he would be to her whatever she needed or wanted—father, mother, brother, or even husband; he would plan for and about her, care for her.

He found himself unexpectedly smiling at himself in mirrors. He'd found a new thing to believe in. Maybe this time he'd perform better. Maybe this time he'd not let it scream and burn and die.

Eighteen days later he was released, the indictment having been dismissed by a judge who'd read the transcript of grand jury testimony and listened to a sheriff who'd testified that Morgan was apparently, from his observations, not a drug addict and not an alcoholic; that he'd at first thought Morgan was, but now did not think so.

Morgan went back to the hospital.

There were ways to do things and ways not to do them. Morgan knew if he vanished with Kelly, there'd be a hue and cry, there'd be a search. That was the way of the system. He found a willing lawyer and filed quiet papers in the court of the same judge who had dismissed the criminal case against him. Morgan worked hard at his job, creating no waves, no controversy. He was offered a permanent appointment and refused it.

He adopted Kelly.

Then they moved on.

Each day he read the news to her. He told her what he could about famous people and powerful governments and about the rich and the deprived. As he read to her, he sometimes wondered whom she'd change and who would die. He supposed it depended more on what she saw than on what he read to her. She seemed bored but tolerant about the reading. He read to her anyway.

They spent that first experimental winter in Washington, and announced a world tour after the critics saw and commented excitedly on Kelly's splendid unexpected work with the heads of the President and his cabinet.

Decision

By his tenth year on the bench, Judge Cleve Marshall had become a judge's judge. His decisions were sought after all over his area of the state. Bright lawyers filed change-of-venue motions and requested him. Life was interesting and busy. He had never married and now, at forty-three, thought he never would. There had been women, and still were, in and around the small town of Avalon where he'd lived all his life. He maintained an active lifestyle. He played fair golf and better tennis. But much of his time was spent, black-robed, listening intently to evidence, studying casebooks for precedent, or mulling over knotty decisions.

He wasn't surprised, therefore, when he was chosen to hear the Fielder murder case: He'd read about it in the area papers and wondered if it would fall to him to sit as presiding judge in it. He *was* surprised, however, when Prosecutor Hanks and Defense Attorney Baron announced to him, at an omnibus hearing, that he'd hear it without jury.

"Now hold on, boys," he said. "I know and admire both of you and I've read a bit about the case in the local paper. I can maybe see one of you wanting a non-jury trial, but not both of you."

Lester Baron rose and smiled at him. "Judge, this woman is accused of deliberately poisoning her husband and daughter. My feeling is that a jury would be swayed by the mere fact she's accused, would disregard the flimsiness of the evidence, and would want to punish Alice Fielder because her husband and child are dead. So I'm asking that you alone hear it. My client has agreed."

George Hanks nodded. "The prosecution is willing to go along because the evidence is circumstantial, with inferences arising out of inferences. We think it requires a judicial mind to realize the full perfidy of what Alice Fielder did to her family." He smiled like a half-open knife. He'd always been an effective but vicious prosecutor.

"So be it then," Judge Marshall said. "How long do you foresee it will take to try the matter, gentlemen?"

"A few days. Certainly no more than a week," Baron said. "Much of the evidence could even be stipulated, but won't be because of a circumstance. That circumstance is, of course, a separate page asking for the death penalty. Prosecutor Hanks is also willing to go along because of that possibility. Mrs. Fielder is a very handsome woman. He believes a jury might convict her but not sentence her to death. And he wants the death penalty."

Hanks nodded. "Will you do it, Judge?"

Cleve Marshall folded his hands. "I've never turned down a case, but I want both of you to know I'd like to turn this one down. My difficulty is that I can find no reason in the judicial code of ethics why I should."

They set a June trial date.

"One more thing, Judge," Baron said. "Do you know Alice Fielder?"

"Not to my knowledge. If she grew up around here, I *might* know her. I vaguely knew her deceased husband."

"She was a Linip before she was married," Hanks told him.

"I don't remember the name," Marshall said. "I still might know her, but it doesn't mean anything to me. If I find out anything which might bias me before trial, I'll get out."

Both lawyers nodded, satisfied.

After they'd gone, Judge Marshall read the file. There wasn't much there to satisfy his aroused curiosity. There was the information charging Alice Fielder with killing her husband and daughter. There were some discovery motions from both sides and lists of witnesses, most of them the expected people—the police officers who'd made the original run to the Fielder home after the frantic call from Alice Fielder, doctors who'd examined the bodies, a toxicologist who'd run tests on body fluids, some neighbors.

If the prosecution was correct, Alice Fielder had poisoned her husband and fifteen-year-old daughter. Judge Marshall wondered what kind of monster could do that. Then, in the middle of the file, he came across two police photos of Alice Fielder, one taken front face, the other from the side. She was a most pleasant-looking woman, not yet forty. Her face seemed vaguely familiar to him. He tried to remember why, but nothing came. He got his magnifying glass out of his desk and studied the face, giving particular attention to the eyes. They stared at the camera. He couldn't tell whether they were sorrowful, bewildered, or merely cunning. It still seemed as if somewhere, sometime long ago, he'd seen it—and forgotten it.

Dr. Leybeck was an aging medical-expert boor. Marshall had heard him many times and had once stated, only half in joke, that the man could put a jury to sleep while describing the results of an ax murder. Leybeck was a forensic pathologist much used by the prosecutor.

When the veteran police officer who'd made the run had seen the two victims, he'd called Dr. Leybeck and he had arrived on the scene in the company of the coroner.

"The poison was nicotine, pure nicotine, distilled somehow either from some old pesticides we found in a shed outside the house or from tobacco itself. Edgar Fielder managed a tobacco warehouse and it was the height of the season when it happened. Both victims were found in their bedrooms. The dishes from a table in the dining room had been removed, but traces of the poison were found in the food remaining on two of the dinner plates. The family had eaten some sort of Mexican meal, very hot and spicy. After Sergeant Jones read her Mirandas to her, Mrs. Fielder said it was enchiladas and she had prepared it."

"What effect would nicotine have upon someone who ingested it?" the prosecutor asked.

"A fatal dose could be as little as one drop. It would first stimulate, then depress the cells of peripheral autonomic ganglia, particularly the midbrain, and the spinal cord. Initially, there'd be a burning of the mouth, throat, and stomach, then nausea, tachycardia, elevation of blood pressure, respiratory slowing, coma, and finally death. These symptoms would follow each other with great rapidity. And from my tests, that's how Edgar and Joan Fielder died." The doctor stared out into the warm, crowded courtroom. It was almost full. Murder cases still drew crowds.

"Did you do tests on the plates found in Mrs. Fielder's kitchen?"

"Yes."

"And the results?"

"The food on them was liberally doused with pure nicotine. Enough to kill ten people. I estimated a time of death for each victim about ten to thirty minutes after the drug was ingested."

Lester Baron asked on cross examination: "You saw nothing in the house to indicate that Mrs. Fielder had prepared some sort of apparatus to distill pure nicotine?"

"No. I didn't look."

After Dr. Leybeck, there came a parade of neighbors and acquaintances of the Fielders. They testified concerning public quarrels and threats. Close neighbors testified to the sounds of strife emanating almost constantly from the Fielder home and to occasional marks they'd seen on Mrs. Fielder after the battles. Once her arm had been broken. Once she'd apparently scalded her husband so severely with hot coffee that he'd been laid up for a week. The daughter had sometimes come to school with bruises and lacerations.

The most telling witness for the prosecution was a next door neighbor, Janet Robbins. She and Mrs. Fielder were close.

"She said one day she was going to kill Edgar," Mrs. Robbins said.

"Did she say it more than once?"

"Oh, yes. Many times—every time they had a fight. He was always picking on her or the daughter. Joan ran away several times, but was found and sent back home."

Coworkers at the warehouse testified that Mrs. Fielder had been in and out of the place many times and that she and her husband had had arguments there. They attested to Mrs. Fielder's interest in tobacco and the availability of raw tobacco leaves in the warehouse. As one coworker described an attempt she'd made to hit Fielder with a hammer while at the warehouse, Judge Marshall studied the woman from the bench.

She seemed calm enough now. She was wearing inexpensive clothes and smiled only when her lawyer asked a telling cross-question. Her features were good, her teeth perfect. She had apparently been difficult to live with, and yet it seemed to have been a two-way street she and her now deceased husband had so tempestuously ridden upon. He'd hurt her and she'd hurt him in return. The daughter had probably been dominated and kept in fear by both of them, but there were questions about that which weren't being asked and that puzzled him.

A teacher had said of her: "She was kind of withdrawn and strange, you know? She was bright enough in some areas, uninterested in others. Her grades ran from F's to A's. She liked science and reading. Until around the time she died, she was like a little girl, though she'd matured physically over the last summer vacation. She didn't take part in any of the extra-curricular activities at the school. She read a lot—those dreadful things they write for young adults now. She came to school, she went home. She was a pretty child, but she seemed afraid of boys. Several times she broke down and cried in class. I took her aside and asked her if she was ever beaten at home, but she'd never admit it to me or any of the other teachers, even when she came to school with bruises."

Police Sergeant Jones testified about going to the house and finding the two bodies in the bedrooms. When he had arrived, Mrs. Fielder had shown almost no emotion. She'd politely invited him inside the quiet house, saying her husband and daughter had gotten sick after supper and were in bed. She willingly allowed Jones to enter the bedrooms where he'd found the still-warm bodies.

"I read her the Miranda warning and she said she'd fixed the meal. When I asked her other questions, she said she'd like to have a lawyer first so I stopped."

"Did you search the house?"

"Yes, later. That's when we found the poison on the closet shelf in her bedroom, sitting right out in plain sight."

"Did you find anything to indicate that it had been distilled inside the house?"

"There were some old chemistry things down in the basement—you know, bottles and retorts and tubing. One of

161

those kid sets you can buy in a toy store. We analyzed them, but they were clean. I checked the local night school and found out Mrs. Fielder had taken some chemistry courses there, but I don't know if the stuff we found in the basement was hers or her daughter's." He shrugged. "Or her husband's."

A teacher from the night school testified that Mrs. Fielder had taken enough courses to understand how to distill the poison and would be likely to know of its highly toxic nature. Avalon was a tobacco town and workers in the warehouses had suffered chronic, but curable, poisoning, and those poisonings had been reported in the local newspaper.

The prosecution rested.

Defense Counsel Baron made the obligatory motion for judgment and Marshall politely overruled it, pointing out that there'd been three people in the Fielder house, that two of them were dead, and that a prima facie case had been established.

"You may begin your evidence," he said.

Baron nodded and went back to the defense table. For a time he and his client held a low-voiced discussion—seemingly amiable until Marshall saw that Baron was becoming red-faced and somewhat angry.

Finally, Baron approached the bench. "Could we break until tomorrow morning? I need to talk with my client concerning her defense."

George Hanks got to his feet. "I'll have to object, Your Honor," he said smoothly. "Mr. Baron and his client have had some months to prepare strategy."

Marshall nodded and looked at his watch. It was almost four. "True, but I'll give Mr. Baron until the morning."

At the courtroom door, Marshall saw Alice Fielder look back at him—calculating him, perhaps. A tiny memory came and again he thought he might barely remember her. There had been a time after his freshman year in college when he'd summered as a lifeguard at the local municipal pool. There had been dozens of girls around that summer, some older than he was, some his age, many younger. He thought he remembered a face like Alice Fielder's somewhere in that lost crowd. He wondered if she'd been one of his "summer girls." It had been a lot of years.

In the morning, a sullen Baron rested without introducing any evidence. The two lawyers made closing argument and Marshall returned the defendant to the dirty, aging county jail while he considered the case.

For days, he sat in his law library, smelling the dampness and decay and rereading his casebooks. He vacillated. Sometimes he was sure Alice Fielder was guilty but at other times he was not. He did know that two people had died and that a third who'd been present had not and that that was strong circumstantial evidence.

On a day in early July he ordered the court back into session. The prosecutor came smiling into the courtroom and the defense counsel arrived scowling. Neither expression lasted long.

"I find," Marshall announced, "after careful consideration, that there is insufficient evidence against the defendant to convict Mrs. Fielder of murder. At times, in considering this case, I have had the feeling that the defendant probably committed the crime, but I have never been able to say to myself, beyond a reasonable doubt, that she committed the double murder of her husband and daughter. Therefore, I now order that she be released from custody."

He nodded down at the deputy who was guarding Alice Fielder. "I'm sure she has personal belongings at the jail.

163

Return her there and allow her to pick them up." He nodded at her. "You're free, Mrs. Fielder. I hope I've done the right thing. I know I've done the legally right thing."

She nodded back at him, not smiling. There were tears in her eyes. It was the first sign of strong emotion he'd observed in her.

He didn't see Alice Fielder for some months after the trial. Lester Baron told him she'd gone off somewhere to escape the publicity. There had been a substantial amount. Marshall had caught the brunt of it, smiling and repeating "Insufficient evidence" until the public interest finally moved on to fresher news.

He encountered her at a restaurant he favored. He'd never seen her there before. She sat at the bar, drinking a tall icy drink, wearing a tailored dress that set off her figure and face far better than the drab apparel she'd worn in the courtroom. Her eyes were as he remembered them, lost and forlorn, and it struck him that, strangely enough, she might be there hoping to speak with him.

"I see you survived my release," she said when he went over to her. "I want to thank you for it." She smiled without humor. "Some in town still think I'm guilty. I'm about to move away; I've given up hope for a normal life here."

He nodded and waited, sensing she wanted to say more.

"Why did you find me innocent?" she asked. "My lawyer was sure you wouldn't when I refused to take the witness stand."

"You had a constitutional right not to testify," Marshall said. "I found you not guilty because I could see another way the deaths could have happened. Your husband could have poisoned the plates and then gotten a poisoned one by mistake, having meant the poison for you and your daughter.

You have studied chemistry, so I didn't think you would leave plates with poison on them in the sink until the police came, invite the police officer in, admit you prepared the dinner, and let him enter the bedrooms without objection." He shook his head. "The only thing that puzzled me about the trial is why you yourself didn't say on the witness stand what I'm saying now."

She smiled. "There was a reason. And you have a right to know. I wasn't going to get on the witness stand and tell what happened, not even if I had to die for it, but I'll tell you if you promise you'll tell no one else. I want you to know and understand."

He nodded, his curiosity aroused. Besides, he found himself attracted to her. He knew she couldn't be for him, but he was still attracted. "You were one of my summer girls, weren't you?"

She nodded. "I didn't think you remembered that."

"It took me a while," he admitted.

She looked into her glass, her face somber again.

"He always beat on us. Maybe it was something that went wrong in his childhood. I could take his viciousness to me, but he was also vicious to Joan. I threw that scalding coffee on him when he was beating her, not me. I could take care of myself, she couldn't. I was physically about as strong as he was. Then, when Joan started to grow up, he changed subtly toward her. He patted her and kissed her and she didn't know how to handle that. It got worse. What he did damaged her.

"Joan carried the plates to the table that night. She must have distilled the poison. The chemistry set was hers; I bought it for her one Christmas when she was about twelve. She was very good at things like chemistry and physics. I heard her tinkering with the set in the basement again in the weeks before it happened and I saw evidence down there that she was distilling something. It never occurred to me . . ."

"One never suspects the obvious," Marshall said. "Or the very young."

"Yes." She nodded. "And I wanted it kept like that. I remembered your kindness when you were a lifeguard. You never really saw me that summer, but I saw you. I loved you that summer I was only fourteen and you were eighteen or nineteen. Love's very difficult at that age. Joan's age. I couldn't sit in your court and say that my sexually brutalized daughter had poisoned her father and herself. I doubted I'd be believed anyway, but whether I was believed or not I couldn't make myself do it. I couldn't for her and I couldn't for me. They were both dead and it was over.

"But I want you personally to know before I move on that you made the right decision. If you can keep it secret I'll be very grateful."

"Where will you go?"

"Someplace new."

He smiled at her. "Stay in touch with me."

"All right." She set the unfinished drink down and got up as if to leave. She looked at him and said again, "All right."

Truly Yours, John R. Jacks

There was a full November moon up there in the night sky and Jacks, who kept up on things like that, knew it, but the moon was dimmed by thin, late-fall clouds. He pressed a button on the luxury car's dash and a computer readout told him it was thirty degrees outside. *Cold.*

He liked the big car and the feeling of power it gave him. It seemed almost an extension of himself. He pushed the accelerator down a little and tasted the added speed.

The road ahead appeared deserted, but then Jacks saw the hitchhiker. He'd read in area newspapers that it wasn't safe or smart to pick them up, especially on semi-deserted roads, but he'd done it before. And it was an unusually cold night for anyone to be out. He slowed.

The man who opened the passenger door of the Cadillac was thin and gray, older in appearance than Jacks. He was dressed in worn jeans and wore a thick but threadbare coat. He smiled ingratiatingly.

"Thanks," he said, climbing in. He smelled vaguely of mothballs and burning leaves. "For a while I didn't think anyone would ever pick me up. Not much traffic on this road, what with all the interstates nearby. Nice of a young man like you to pick up an old man like me."

"I'm going as far as Bargersville," Jacks said, smiling back. He nodded at the backseat of his car. "I sell supplies to hospitals, emergency rooms, and doctors all over five states and I wanted to get to Bargersville tonight so I could make an early start in the morning. You can make better time on the back roads this time of year. And they're far more interesting to drive."

"Drug salesman?" the man asked.

"No. Equipment. Small stuff, retractors, clamps, scalpel blades." He smiled. "If I was into selling drugs I'd never pick anyone up." He extended his right hand. "Name's Jacks, John R. Jacks."

The other man nodded and shook hands, his own hand cold in Jacks's warm palm. "I'm Joe Bell. Your accent sounds British."

"So it is a bit," Jacks said, surprised at the man's acuteness. "I was born and raised in the east part of the finest city in the world, London, but I've been all over. One never loses one's birth heritage, I suppose."

"I've lived a lot of places, too," Bell said. "Some of them not very nice. Hospitals. Rest homes. That sort of thing." His voice was bitter.

Jacks nodded politely while Bell settled deeper into the passenger seat of the Cadillac.

Jacks got the car rolling well again, seeing the speedometer pass fifty miles an hour. "Beastly night to be hitchhiking."

Bell smiled sleepily and nodded. "I guess I'm a bit more than your average hitchhiker." He put his right hand casually in his coat pocket and brought out a small revolver. "I do people for a hobby—men, women, kids, it makes me no difference." He looked out at the road ahead. "About a mile or so up there's a side road that I know. You pull in there. Then you and I will have a bit of fun before I leave you behind and take your car. Maybe with it I can get away from here, away from where they're undoubtedly already looking for me, although I've only been gone for a day or so."

"They're looking for you?" Jacks asked.

Bell nodded. "Yes. You're a real saviour."

"What sort of fun are you after?" Jacks asked.

"You'll do things for me and I'll do things to you," Bell said. "Great fun. I'll like it. You may not. One never knows about pretty young men like you." His lip curled.

Jacks nodded, understanding. The spring knife he kept up his right sleeve, ready to flick down at the right movement, felt warm and good against his skin. The juices inside him quickened. Perhaps there'd be a chance.

"I take it you've engaged in this sort of antisocial conduct before?" he asked in a low voice, scandalized by the thought of it.

"Many times," Bell said. He shrugged, his attitude almost apologetic. "They lock me up when they catch me, but I'm difficult to catch and hard to hold. They say I'm insane, but I know I'm not. One doctor said what I did was an irresistible impulse. I liked the phrase when I heard it. I'm afraid my impulse is something I just have to do now and then. It was very kind of you to stop for me. Now I'm going to repay you."

"I don't want repayment," Jacks said. "You can take the car and what's in it. Just let me go, let me out. I won't say anything to anyone."

"But I must repay you," Bell answered mockingly.

They drove on. In the other lane a car approached, the first one Jacks had seen in the better part of an hour. There were lights mounted on the top of the approaching vehicle.

"Careful now," Bell said. "That's a state police car. Do anything wrong and I'll shoot you now and spoil all our fun-to-be."

Jacks shook his head. "I'm not even tempted." He drove steadily onward. He nodded curiously at Bell. "But think about it yourself. What would or could you do if I drove my auto into the other lane? If you shot me you'd probably die also in the crash. Or the police would have caught you."

"Don't be silly. You'd die too."

"Realistic is the way I view it," Jacks pointed out. "I doubt you intend me to live through this anyway."

They drove on in silence. Bell watched Jacks carefully, perhaps not as sure of him as he'd been at first. Jacks smiled at him to lull him back to a sense of security.

"You don't seem afraid," Bell said. "You should be praying."

"I gave up praying years ago," Jacks said. "I'm a fatalist. What will be will be. Shouldn't your mile be about up?"

"There's the side road now," Bell said pointing, then looking quickly back at Jacks, watching him carefully.

"Yes," Jacks said. "I see it." He pulled into a narrow lane and drove bumpily back about fifty feet from the highway.

"Far enough," Bell said, excited again now. "Park the car right here. Get out on your side. Don't try to run. I'm very good with this gun."

"I'm sure you would be," said Jacks. He turned off his lights and opened his door carefully. He got out of the car. Even with the full moon behind thin clouds there was enough light to see. It was very cold, but the wind was still. Jacks smelled the coming of winter. Someplace close by an owl called its greeting to the two interlopers into its frigid world.

Jacks triggered the closed spring knife down into his hand. There was a button on top of it which let the blade slide down from inside the handle. He'd seen it in a small shop in Germany, liked it, and bought it. Years ago.

"Come around here to me," Bell said whiningly, quite excited now. "Come see the last of your life. Come to me."

Jacks complied docilely.

"Come close," Bell ordered. "So pretty," he crooned.

Jacks moved closer. He saw that the gun had vanished

back into a pocket and that Bell now menacingly held a short pocket knife.

"I'm going to penetrate you a little and then there'll be your clothes to be removed," Bell whispered. He moved lovingly forward. "Be good," he pleaded. He raised the knife hesitantly. "Some of them just die. Don't do that. Fun first."

Jacks waited motionless until Bell was very close. Then he pressed the handle button and heard the tiny snicking sound. He brought the long knife up swiftly so that it pressured the hollow under Bell's jaw. He countered Bell's thrust with his free hand, locking Bell's arm. Bell looked at him with shocked eyes. Jacks let the point of his long knife dig in a quarter of an inch, drawing blood.

"Make me uneasy in any way and I'll let this blade glide up through your tongue and into your brain," Jacks said. "You can already feel that it's very sharp, not like the dirty thing you carry." He smiled at Bell. "You drop your little toy and then take off your coat. That will put your revolver beyond your immediate reach should you be tempted to try to use it."

Bell followed the instructions. He stood shivering in the cold, a thin old man out on a night much too cold for lam, still excited, but now in a different way.

"If you're going to turn me in there's a police station in Bargersville. In a few weeks I'd probably have turned myself in anyway. It's getting too cold to stay out long. Next time I'll try to remember to escape in the summer. They watch me close for a while and then they forget." He smiled. "And away I go."

Jacks nodded, not very much interested.

"You turn me in and they'll take me back to the asylum," Bell said conversationally. He smiled. "It's not so bad there and maybe I'll get out again. I have my scrapbook at the asylum for the lonely, cold nights. I keep it hidden so that only I get to see it. Lots of lovely news clips. Some about me, some about others like me." He nodded, agitated a little. "It's very cold without my coat. Can't we get back in the car now?"

"Maybe in a few moments," Jacks said. "I'd wager you would get out again, but I'm not going to turn you in. I haven't got the time or the inclination to come back for hearings and perhaps a trial." Jacks shook his head. "Gentlemen like you are a hazard." He pointed out at the Cadillac. "My vehicle is parked so close to the road that if that state chap who was going the other way came back and drove past he'd likely see it and us."

"I've used this place before and not been caught," Bell said. "Back in the bushes there's a body from yesterday. Would you like to see it? Very nice body. An old, talkative lady."

"No," Jacks said.

"You'd have joined her. Then one more. I like to do them in threes. Lucky, you know."

Jacks shook his head in wonder. "And you never bothered to examine me for a weapon. You took me for granted. I'm surprised you've lived as long as you have."

"Most people do what I say," Bell said. "They're too scared and shocked not to do it. They think maybe I'll let them go if they do exactly what I tell them." He moved his head cautiously, not liking the knife at his throat. "That hurts me. Where'd the knife come from? You made it appear like something out of a magic trick."

"From back the years," Jacks said. He shook his head. "Random killers like you, sexual deviates, thrill murderers, psychopaths, give the civilized world a bad odor." He pulled the sharp knife slightly away.

Bell seemed to relax a little as he was able to lower his head. He rubbed the cut spot on his neck, seemingly puzzled by it. He put a bloody fingertip from the wound in his mouth. "It never seems to hurt when they cut each other on TV. Or I never thought it hurt until I killed my first one." He shook his head wonderingly. "She screamed a lot."

Jacks heard a sound approaching from far away. He shoved the knife close to Bell's throat again.

Both of the men stood unmoving while out on the road a truck went past, traveling fast, unseeing, not slowing.

When it was still again, Jacks said calmly and reasonably, "One must learn how, when, and why to kill, how to follow the stars from old books that were banned and burned whenever they were found. I read the last survivor of those old dark god books before it was also destroyed. That was a long time ago. That book taught me how a man could stay young forever. I've followed what it taught. I've lived in a dozen countries. I like this one best. Very easy here, very relaxed. Lots of serial killers to keep the police busy. Lots of violence. I'm going to stay and prosper forever. In a moment I'm going to get my own little kit of sharp, delicate things from among those items in my backseat I sell to doctors and hospitals and emergency rooms."

Bell shook his head. "You can't kill me. Only I can kill." His eyes were positive. "I am the power. No one else can kill, Mr. John R. Jacks, whoever you are."

"I can," Jacks said surely. "You see, I need certain portions of you for my required periodic rituals." He smiled. "I first learned the trade as a young man in London in 1888. Then it was women only, but my sorcery now allows men." He bowed slightly. "I am in your debt. You will be the latest to help me remain forever young."

Bell shrieked once as the sharp knife entered and penetrated.

Jacks said mockingly, the doggerel coming to him instantaneously, as it always had since those early great times in London when he'd written to the newspapers of the times:

"You forgot both Jacks in my name, Mr. Bell,
But those Jacks should have been a sure tipper.
So remember well, as you head for hell,
That the R. in my name stood for 'Ripper.' "

Trial

Senator Adams called me into his office early that morning. He nodded me into an ancient overstuffed chair, parted a place in his lawbooks so that he could peer through at me, and then began. I could sense he wasn't very happy.

"I want you to help me defend Russell Quinn next week, Robak. I'll pick the jury and be with you most of the trial, but I have some problems which may not let me do all the trial with you."

I looked moodily out his sooty window at Bington's fall. Rough winds were blowing varicolored leaves off the courthouse-lawn trees and covering the ground below. The wino crowd, which met daily on the courthouse wall to split a bottle or three of muscatel, weather permitting, seemed unfazed. I wasn't.

"That's *your* murder case," I said uncertainly.

"I see you remember that much about it. It's a start," the senator said sarcastically. A state senator, once elected, later defeated, in my area is "Senator" forever. "Here's the file," he said, handing it to me.

I took it from him. It was bulky. "What's the problem?" I asked, still doubtful.

He looked down at his desk. "I had some chest pains last night and went to the hospital emergency room." He held up a hand. "Nothing real bad, but my doctor ordered me to take it easier. I told him about the trial. The prosecutor and I both want it tried. First the doctor told me to continue it, but Russell has been in jail for seven months. I explained that. So

175

then he ordered me not to try it and have you do it all. I worked out the compromise I'm now spelling out for you."

"All right," I said. I took the file, not happy about it but willing now that all had been revealed. I knew that the senator's health was, at best, questionable. I still didn't much like getting involved late in a murder case and I was still at the stage of my life where I believed people were automatically guilty just because the state had arrested and charged them.

Russell Quinn *was* the local gambler and I knew him a little. He was a big, bulky man with black hair and strong arms. His reputation for peace and sobriety was spotty, but his reputation for tough honesty was first-class. Seven months before he'd been arrested for knifing another local gambler, Odds Jacobson, after an all-night poker game above Jacobson's pool hall. There were no witnesses to the offense itself, but there were other players available from the fatal game who'd heard threats made by Russell to Odds. Odds had won, Russell had lost. Russell had thereupon threatened to kill Odds, accusing him of cheating. Russell's knife was found later by the body. There was no money on the body, but Russell, apprehended at his home, had a wad of cash. Circumstantial, but probably enough.

The senator had made some notes in the file. One of them read, "No Other Enemies?" Another said, "Five Players?" A third was dim and I had to lean down to read it. "Set Up?" it asked.

I went back to his office to ask him about the notes, but he was gone. Virginia, our harassed secretary, said he'd gone home for the day.

I walked back to my own office and reopened the file. There was a list of witnesses for the state. Leaving out the police who'd investigated and the doctors who'd examined

Odds's body, there were only three witnesses who seemed worth investigating: the other three cardplayers.

Senator Adams had already done that. There were depositions inside the file. I read them. They seemed mild enough. They described the card game, the stakes, that Odds had won, and that Russell had lost his money and then his temper. Each cardplayer had stated where he'd gone at the conclusion of the game. The senator had put question marks by two of the names, excepting out only a Sam Shannon. I read the depositions again and thought I might have some idea of the senator's thinking. There were three other suspects, good suspects. All that tied our man Quinn to the case were their statements and the knife.

On the front of the file Senator Adams had printed, "See Coger Rock." Rock was the prosecuting attorney, and a good and fair one.

We began trial on a blustery Tuesday morning. Outside a driving rain scoured Bington's streets. Inside Coger Rock quickly proved that Odds was dead, that the knife found beside him was Russell's property, with his initials on it, and that there'd been bad blood between Odds and Russell. Pictures of a bloody Odds, on a slab, were shown to the jurors. The senator sat beside me, his old prune face calm and seemingly not much interested. On the far side of the counsel table Russell Quinn sat, his face impassive. Now and then he'd make a note on a yellow pad and hand it to the senator. Behind Russell two deputy sheriffs sat watching.

The senator first came a little alive when the state presented a fingerprint expert. He leaned forward and listened to him testify.

"I found a fingerprint on the small blade of the knife," the expert said. "I checked it and it was Russell Quinn's print."

Prosecutor Rock, huge in his best black suit, wheezingly set up a projector and showed the print on the knife blade, then showed the jury another taken from Russell Quinn and had the expert testify learnedly about their sameness. I saw jurors nodding.

Senator Adams leaned to me. "Ask this cookie which blade of the knife killed Odds Jacobson."

I did, politely enough, when Prosecutor Rock was done with his impressive show and tell.

"I don't know," he said haughtily. "All I did was what I was supposed to do—check fingerprints. Those of Russell Quinn were the only ones I found on the knife I examined."

"And that print on the small blade was the only print you found?"

"Yes. There were smudges other places, but no prints."

Dr. Katen, who'd done the autopsy, had the information the senator wanted.

"He was killed with the long blade of the knife. Someone stabbed him five times in and around the heart. The stab wounds were deep, too deep for the short blade, but they fit with the long blade of the knife. Once the blade was withdrawn wounds of that nature contract. Odds's fatal wounds had done that but could not have been the work of the short blade." He nodded. "The wounds would have had to have been made by a strong person."

The jury examined Russell Quinn and saw what they needed as far as strength was concerned.

"How strong?" I asked.

The doctor shrugged. "What I mean by that is that the wounds couldn't have been inflicted by an eighty-year-old woman."

Senator Adams nodded at me, satisfied. "Now we wait until they call the other poker players," he whispered. He reached in his briefcase. "They're strong, too. Here are their arrest records, Robak. Take them home and read them over tonight." He nodded mysteriously. "The prosecutor and I have already been over them."

"Yes, sir," I said.

"You seem happier than you once were about this case," he said, smiling, but only a little.

"I think you have something up your sleeve," I said.

He looked at me and I couldn't read anything in his old lizard eyes. "Read the arrest records. And tomorrow we must warn Judge Steinmetz and the prosecutor that there's a separation of witnesses in effect and that we don't want the witnesses talking among themselves. Perhaps the judge might even put a deputy in the hall to make certain that doesn't happen."

"Why bother?" I asked.

He smiled but would say no more.

I went home to my apartment and read and then re-read the records of the three other witnesses. Reading them was about like going to a seminar on all the various offenses of man. The three had been involved in a variety of crimes.

I kept waking up in the night and going over the cross-examination I planned. Between them the three witnesses had been convicted of everything from manslaughter to pickpocketing. None of the three was clean.

I planned and then slept. I awoke early, when the sun first streaked the sky with light, and went over what I'd read again. Outside the day had awakened cold and there was a hint of snow in the air. I walked to the courthouse.

The first of the three was Sam Shannon. Coger Rock led him through testimony about the game, about Quinn's pique at losing, and about the threats which had been made.

"He said he'd kill Odds. He said Odds had cheated." Shannon nodded righteously, "I didn't see no cheating."

Rock stopped and left him to us. Senator Adams nodded me on and I went after Sam Shannon.

"Did you ever threaten Odds Jacobson, Mr. Shannon?"

"Not me. I try to get along with everyone."

"Did you get along with one Edward Black on or about the eighth day of April five years ago?"

"Objection," Coger said for the record. We'd already argued out what was available to us in evidence in a hearing out of the presence of the jury earlier. And Rock and the senator had both seemed very friendly about their arguments, which was a bit unusual.

"You may answer," Judge Steinmetz said, looking down.

"Me and Eddo had some problems. I did my time for that."

"Didn't you attack Edward Black with a knife on that date and kill him?"

"Sure, but it was a fair fight."

"Did Odds Jacobson fight fair when you took Quinn's knife to him the night you killed him?" I asked.

"I never did it to him. Me and Odds was friends. Ask anyone."

"Did you leave Odds's premises with the other two players in the game besides Odds and Quinn Russell?"

"No. They went their way, I went mine. We're not that close."

I couldn't get him to change anything. I tried various devices, trying to trap him, but nothing worked. Finally I caught the senator's nod and went to the counsel table.

"Enough," he whispered. "This one has a good alibi for the rest of that evening. Three people came by and picked him up at the pool hall when the game was over and were with him the rest of the night. Ask for a short recess."

I looked up at Steinmetz. "Could we have five minutes to confer before the next witness is called, Your Honor?"

"All right," Judge Steinmetz said, looking at us curiously.

When the jury had gone out Senator Adams asked, "Do you think you can figure a way to make the next witness very angry at you, Robak?"

"I can try." I looked around the old courtroom, thinking about it. Making people mad was one of my gifts.

"Keep working on him until you do. Be your normal self, nasty, sarcastic, disagreeable. Accuse him, confront him, and make him angry at you. I'm told he has a hair-trigger temper."

"Yes, sir," I said, wondering why.

"I want to talk to Coger Rock for a moment now," he said.

I watched him walk over to the other counsel table and confer with Rock, who listened and nodded. The whole thing was confusing to me.

The next witness for the State was Charles "Chuck" Whiteway and what I'd read on him wasn't very encouraging. At one time he'd been a very good daylight burglar in the area in and around Bington. He'd also been a strongarm bandit. He'd gone to prison twice and had spent time in most of the area jails, usually for fighting. Lately he'd seemed to semi-retire, had taken a job as a combination bartender-bouncer in one of Bington's tough bars. He was large and fortyish and moved with great energy and vigor. His eyes seemed to view the world around him with contempt.

Once again Prosecutor Coger Rock led him through the story concerning the poker game and dug it out of him. He seemed reluctant to testify and I thought I'd use that against him.

I got him after an hour of wheedling by Coger.

"You seem reluctant to testify, Mr. Whiteway," I said. "Why is that?"

He nodded at me. "Both Quinn and Odds were friends of mine."

"I'll bet. How did you get to know Odds? In prison?"

"Odds was never in prison, bud."

"I see. Did you get to know him by burglarizing his place? Or maybe beating him up? Or robbing him?"

He shook his head, his face reddening a little.

"And you say Russell Quinn here is or was a friend of yours, too?" I asked.

"That's right."

"Having you for a friend isn't of much help to either one of them. One's dead, the other's here on trial for murder with you testifying against him."

"I was subpoenaed."

"Anybody pay you to be here?"

He pulled at his collar and glared at me. "Of course not."

"You're too honest for that, aren't you?" I asked, grinning superciliously at him.

"I'm honest enough," he said doggedly.

"I don't think there's any truth in you, Mr. Whiteway. I think you stole for so long that it's your way of life. And I think now you're trying to steal—"

It was enough. He came up out of the witness chair and aimed one my way. I ducked inside it and then the bailiff and one of the deputies had him. Steinmetz pounded his gavel.

"Take that man to jail and let him cool off. You can call him back later if you want, Mr. Robak."

I nodded.

At our counsel table Senator Adams looked pleased. I tried to read Coger Rock's expression but couldn't.

We insisted on moving ahead and so Coger called his last

witness, Don Bradberry. He was the youngest of the players and he came through as a very unctuous witness. His record indicated he'd been a sneak thief since his youth, a pickpocket, and a con man. He had earnest blue eyes that he partially hid behind large hornrims. I guessed him to be thirty, tall, built like a football end. Coger finished with him in half an hour.

The senator whispered, "I'll take this one."

I nodded, surprised. He seemed alive again. When the prosecution finished he was on his feet circling Bradberry like some old, still savage bird of prey.

"We've had some startling things happen here today, Mr. Bradberry. The last witness was taken to jail."

Bradberry nodded warily.

"Can you think of any reason for that?"

"No, sir," he said nervously and waited.

"Think hard," the senator said, grinning coldly at him.

Bradberry shrugged.

"Could it be because he told us you stole Russell Quinn's knife, which meant he'd lied in his deposition? Could that be it?"

"If he told you that, he lied," Bradberry said, looking at the senator with hate in his eyes.

"He told us a lot of things," the senator said.

Coger Rock started to get up and then sat back down. He shook his head like a bewildered boxer and glanced down at his counsel table.

Bradberry looked at the senator. "I picked the knife for him. He gave me a hundred for it. He said if I ever told he'd kill me." He shook his head in disgust at the perfidy of men. "And then he breaks and tells. That's all I know."

The senator turned to me and then to the prosecutor. "Enough?" he asked Coger.

The prosecutor nodded.

Later I sat with both of them in the downtown Moose.

"You set me up," I said to both of them.

"Coger wasn't satisfied and neither was I," the senator said. "He agreed to give me a little leeway. He did and here we are." He smiled his sour lemon smile. "No one likes to convict an innocent man. The evidence that Coger had against Russell Quinn was enough to convict with, but not enough to completely convince Coger."

Rock nodded. He drank his diet cola, perspiring freely despite the air conditioning. He smiled at me. "I may never do that sort of thing again. The best man of that bunch of poker players was Russell Quinn. He's mean and a brawler. I thought he might have beaten Odds to death, but not have knifed him. The senator thought, after the depositions, that it was Whiteway. But no one was going to change things without someone tinkering with the process. So I let you guys have a little leeway." He looked at the senator and then at his watch. "It's time," he said.

"Where are you off to?" I asked.

"A poker game at Judge Steinmetz's house. I can promise that none of today's players will be there. Care to join us?"

Shut the Final Door

The night was gentle and so Willie sat out on the combination fire escape and screened play area that hung in zigzags from the north side of the government-built, low-rent apartment building. He stayed out there in his wheelchair for a long time watching the world of lights from the other buildings around him. He liked the night. It softened the savage world, so that he could forget the things he saw and did in the day. Those things still existed, but darkness fogged them.

He reached around, fumbling under his shirt, and let his hand touch the long scar where it started. He couldn't reach all of it for it ran the width of his back, a slanting line, raised from the skin. Sometimes it ached and there was a little of that tonight, but it wasn't really bad anymore. It was only that he was dead below the scar line, that the upper half of him still lived and felt, but the lower felt nothing, did nothing.

Once they'd called him Willie the Runner, and he had been very fast: the running a defense from the cruel world of the apartments, a way out, a thing of which he'd been quite proud. That had been when he was thirteen. Now he was fifteen. The running was gone forever and there was only a scar to remind him of what had been once. But the new gift had come, the one the doctors had hinted about. And those two who'd been responsible for the scar had died.

A cloud passed across the moon and a tiny, soft rain began to fall. He wheeled off the fire escape and into the dirty hall. It was very dark inside. Someone had again removed the light bulbs from their receptacles. Piles of refuse crowded the cor-

185

ners and hungry insects scurried at the vibration of Willie's wheelchair. In the apartment his mother sat in front of the television. Her eyes were open, but she wasn't seeing the picture. She was on something new, exotic. He'd found one of the bottles where she'd carefully hidden it. Dilaudin, or something like that. It treated her well. He worked the wheelchair over to the television and turned off the late-night comic, but she still sat there, eyes open and lost, looking intently at the darkened tube. He went on into his own bedroom, got the wheelchair close to the bed, and clumsily levered himself between the dirty sheets.

He slept and sleeping brought the usual dreams of the days of fear and running. In the dream they laughed coldly and caught him in the dark place and he felt the searing pain of the knife. He remembered the kind doctor in the hospital, the one who kept coming back to talk to him, the one who talked about compensation and factors of recovery. The doctor had told him his arms might grow very strong and agile. He'd told him about blind men who'd developed special senses. He'd smiled and been very nice, and Willie had liked him. The gift he'd promised had come. Time passed in the dream and it became better and Willie smiled.

In the morning, before his mother left for the weekly ordeal with the people at the welfare office, Willie again had her wheel him down to the screened play area and fire escape. In the hall, with the arrival of day, the smell was stifling, a combination of dirt and urine and cooking odors and garbage. The apartments in the building were almost new, but the people who inhabited the apartments had lived in tenement squalor for so long that they soon wore all newness away. The tenants stole the light bulbs from the hallways, used dark corners as toilets of convenience, discarded the leftovers of living in the quickest easiest places. And they fought and stole and raped and, sometimes, killed.

Sometimes, Willie had seen a police car pass in the streets outside, but the policemen usually rode with eyes straight ahead and windows rolled up tight. On the few times that police came into the apartment area they came in squads for their own protection.

Outside the air was better. Willie could see the other government apartments that made up the complex, and if he leaned forward he could, by straining, see the early morning traffic weaving along the expressway by the faraway river.

His mother frowned languidly at the sky, her chocolate-brown face severe. "It'll maybe rain," she said, slurring the words together. "If it rains you get back in, hear?"

"Okay," he said, and then again, because he was never sure she heard him, "Okay!" He looked at her swollen, sullen face, wanting to say more, but no words came. She was so very young. He'd been born almost in her childhood and there was within him the feeling that she resented him, hated caring for him, abominated being tied to him, but did the dreary duty only because there was no one else and because the mother-feeling within warred with all the other wants and drives and sometimes won an occasional victory. Willie remembered no father, and his mother had never spoken of one.

"None of them bad kids bother you up here, do they?" she asked, always suspicious.

He smiled, really amused. "No," he said.

She shook her head tiredly and he noticed the twitch in the side of her dark face. She said, "Some of them's bad enough to bother around a fifteen-year-old boy in a wheelchair. Bad enough to do 'most anything I guess. When we moved in here I thought it would be better." She looked up at

187

the sky. "It's worse," she ended softly.

Willie patiently waited out her automatic ministrations, the poking at the blanket around his wasting legs, the peck on the forehead. Finally, she left.

For a while then he was alone and he could crane and watch the expressway and the river and the downtown to the north. He could hear the complex around him come to angry life, the voices raised in argument and strife. Down below four boys came out of a neighboring building. They were dressed alike, tight jeans, brown jackets, hair long. He saw them gather in front of the building and one of them looked up and saw him watching. That one nudged the others and they all looked up, startled, and they went away like deer, around the far corner of their building at a quick lope. Willie only nodded.

A block away, just within his vision, a tall boy came out of the shadows and engaged another boy in a shouting argument. A small crowd gathered and watched indolently, some yelling advice. Willie watched with interest. When the fight began they rolled out of sight and Willie could only see the edges of the milling crowd and soon lost interest in watching.

The sun came out and the sky lightened and Willie felt more like facing the day. He looked down at his legs without real sorrow. Regret was an old acquaintance, the feeling between them no longer strong. Willie leaned back in the wheelchair. With trained ears alert to any sudden sound of danger, he dozed lightly.

Memory again became a dream. When he had become sure of the gift he had followed them to their clubhouse. It was in a ruined building that the city was tearing down to build more of the interminable housing units. He rolled right up to the door and beat on it boldly and they came and he saw the surprise on their faces and their quick looks to see if he'd brought police along.

"Hello, Running Willie, you crippled bastard," the one who'd wielded the knife said. The one who'd held him and watched smiled insolently.

He sat there alone in the chair and looked back at them, hating them with that peculiar, complete intensity, wanting them dead. The sickness came in his stomach and the whirling in his head and he saw them move at him before the sunlit world went dark brown.

Now they were dead.

A door opened below and Willie came warily awake. He looked down and saw Twig Roberts observing the day.

"Okay to come on up, Willie?" Twig asked carefully.

"Sure," Willie said negligently.

Twig came up the stairs slowly and sat down on the top one, looking away into the distance, refusing to meet Willie's eyes. He was a large, dark boy, muscled like a wrestler, with a quick, foxy face. He lived in the apartment below Willie's.

"What we goin' to do today, Willie boy?" Twig asked it softly, his voice a whine. "Where we headin'?" He continued to look out at the empty sky and Willie knew again that Twig feared him. A small part of Willie relished the fear and fed on it, and Willie knew that the fear diminished both of them.

Willie thought about the day. Once the trips, the forays, into that wild, jackdaw land below had been an exciting thing, a thing of danger. That had been when the power was unsure and slow, but the trips were as nothing now. Instead of finding fear below he brought it.

He said softly, "We'll do something, Twig." Then he nodded, feeling small malice. "Maybe down at Building Nineteen. You been complaining about Building Nineteen, ain't you?" He smiled, hiding the malice. "You got someone down there for me?"

Twig looked at him for the first time. "You got it wrong, Willie. I got relatives in that building. I never even taken you around there for fear . . ." He stopped and then went on. "There's nothing wrong with Nineteen." He watched earnestly until Willie let his smile widen. "You were puttin' me on, Willie," Twig said, in careful half-reproach.

"Sure, Twig," Willie said, closing his eyes and leaning back in the wheelchair. "We'll go down and just sort of look around."

The fan in the elevator didn't work and hadn't worked for a long time, but at least today the elevator itself worked. The odor in the shaft was almost overpowering and Willie was glad when they were outside in the bright sun that had eaten away the morning fog.

Twig maneuvered him out the back entrance of the building. Outside the ground was covered with litter, despite the fact that there were numerous trash receptacles. A rat wheeled and flashed between garbage cans and Willie shivered. The running rat reminded Willie of the days of fear.

They moved on along the sidewalks, Willie in the chair, Twig dutifully behind. Ahead of them Willie could almost feel the word spread. The cool boys vanished. The gangs hid in trembling fear, their zip guns and knives forgotten. Arguments quieted. In the graveled play yards the rough games suspended. Small children watched in wonder from behind convenient bushes, eyes wide. Willie smiled and waved at them, but no one came out. Once a rock came toward them, but when Willie turned there was no one to be seen. There was a dead zone where they walked. It was always like that these days.

A queer thought came to Willie as he rode along in solitary

patrol. It was an odd thought, shiny and unreal. He wondered if someplace there was a someone with the gift of life, a someone who could set stopped breath to moving again, bring color back to a bloodless face, restart a failed heart, bring thought back to a dead mind. He rather hoped that such a gift existed, but he knew that on these streets such a gift wouldn't last. In this filth, in this world of murderous intent the life-giver would have been torn apart. If the life-giver was Willie—if that had been the gift—they would have jerked him from the moving casket he rode, stomped him, mutilated him. And laughed.

There were other worlds. Willie knew that dimly, without remembrance, without real awareness. There was only a kind of dim longing. He knew that the legs were the things that had saved him from a thousand dangers. He remembered the leering man who'd followed him one day when he was twelve, the one who wanted something, who touched and took. He remembered the angry ones with their knives and bicycle chains, the gangs that banded together to spread, rather than absorb, terror. He looked at his world: the ones who'd roll you for the price of a drink and the ones who'd kill you for a fix. It was the only world he knew. Downtown was a thing of minutes spent. It wasn't life. Life was here.

The legs had been survival. A knife had taken them. The doctor had promised something and Willie had believed. Survival was still necessary and the world savage.

So was the compensating gift.

Twig pushed on into a narrow alley between trashcans. The sound of their coming disturbed an old white man who was dirtily burrowing in one of the cans. He looked up at them, filthy hands still rooting in the can. His thin, knobby-armed body seemed lost in indecision between whether to dig deeper in the muck or take flight. Hunger won.

"What you doin' there, man?" Twig demanded, instantly pugnacious at the sight of the dirty, white face.

The old man stood his ground stubbornly and Willie felt an almost empathy with him, remembering hungry days. The man's old eyes were cunning, the head a turtle's head, scrawnily protruding up from its shell of filthy clothing. Those eyes had run a thousand times from imagined terror, but they could still calculate chances. Those eyes saw only a boy in a wheelchair, a larger boy behind.

The old man reached in his pocket. "Ge' away, you li'l black bassurds. Ge' away fum me." The hand came out and there was a flash of dull metal. A knife.

Willie saw Twig smile triumphantly. Those who stood their ground were hard to find in these days of increasing fear.

"Hate him, Willie," Twig said softly. "Hate him now!"

Willie smiled at the old man and hated him without dislike. He had to concentrate very hard, but finally the wrenching, tearing feeling came in his head and the brownout and the sickness became all. He faded himself into the hate and became one with it, and time stopped until there was nothing. When it was done and he was again aware he opened his eyes.

The old man was gone. There was nothing left to show he'd ever existed, no clothes, no knife.

"Did he run?" Willie asked.

Twig shook his head. "He smoked," he said, smiling hugely. "That was the best one yet. He smoked a kind of brown smoke and there was a big puff of flame, and suddenly he ain't there anymore." He cocked his head, and clapped his hands in false exuberance. "That one was good, Willie. It was sure good." He smiled a good smile that failed to reach his eyes.

The sun was warm and Willie sat there and knew he'd

been alone for all fifteen of his years and now, with the gift, that he could remain alone and that he was quite sanely mad.

He looked again at the children playing their rough games in the measured gravel and he knew he could explode them all like toy balloons, but the insanity he owned, he realized, should be worse than that.

The sun remained warm and he contemplated it and thought about it and wondered how far the gift extended. *If I should hate the sun . . .*

There was another thought. He worked it over in his head for a long time, while his fingers absently reached and stroked the long scar on his back.

There was a way out, a possible escape.

Tomorrow he might try hating himself.

The Retiree

In the months following the election in which Judge John Walton was "retired" by the voters, he grew accustomed to having lost, if far from content. There was, of course, less money. He had his retirement pension and that was about all. Most of the money set aside for old age had gone into the doomed fight to save Mary, his deceased wife, from cancer two years back.

Partly to cut expenses and partly because of his quest he moved into the Canning area of the city, called that because once, years back, it had been alive with canning factories. Now the area, close by the river, was a squalid clump of old houses, abandoned factories, and boarded-up stores. It was also the area that "the Butcher" had terrorized.

Walton's apartment was on the second floor of a crumbling brownstone. Living in it was a constant fight against the weather, thieves, and the eternal roaches. But the apartment was large and there was a dry central room for his library of classics. It was also close to a shopping center and the huge magazine store there which stocked out-of-town newspapers.

He grew a beard to protect himself from recognition. It came in thick and gray-white. He found he could pass some people on the street or in a store who'd known him well and not have them recognize him.

Captain Richey visited him in early March, two months plus after Walton's last day in office, four months after he'd moved. They were thirty-year friends dating back to the days when Walton had been a tough deputy prosecutor and Richey an able beat cop.

"This place is the pit of pits," Richey said, looking around the apartment without admiration. "The neighborhood out there is downright dangerous." He shook his head sourly. "I felt like loosening my gun when I parked in front."

Walton smiled. "The apartment's cheap and big and not that bad, Dee." He and Dee Richey had grown closer as they grew older. Richey's wife had died at about the same time as Walton's from the same dread disease. They'd mourned together and become stronger because of shared misery. At times they'd also drunk together, usually too much, but Walton was trying to keep liquor out of the apartment now, knowing his problem and knowing that the problem interfered with his quest. So he'd not offered Richey a drink and they were both becoming uncomfortably aware of it.

"I heard around you had invitations to join law firms. You could have stayed in your old apartment, taken a cushy job, sat around, and looked important." Richey looked at the high stack of newspapers beside Walton's chair. "Can I guess about what you're doing?"

"If you want."

"You still won't admit that the Gracey kid killed those oldies and bums around here. That case got you beat last year, but it didn't cure your stubbornness. So one reason you moved here was to check out things, get close to the scene of the crimes." He shook his head regretfully. "All you had to do in that trial was give that punk the death penalty he deserved and you'd still be on the bench. The jury recommended it. When you didn't follow that recommendation the newspapers got on you, said you were soft and too old, which is a laugh. You're about as soft as an Arizona cactus and you're not much older than me. But the voters read the papers and remembered them on election day and kicked you out."

195

"I believed Gracey's story."

"That he came on a fresh body and was only robbing it? Bull and double bull."

Walton nodded. "He was on hard drugs. I thought it could have been the way he said it was. I even thought it was more likely than not that it was that way. He'd never been involved in a violent crime before. And his story checked out on some of the earlier killings. They never did tie him to anything else."

Richey shrugged. "If he was only a druggie he was a very dumb druggie. And you were a very dumb judge for believing him. You couldn't suspend his sentence because it wasn't suspendable, but you gave him the shortest term of years you could. How come, since you sent him to jail, there've been no more mutilation killings?"

"There have been."

Captain Richey shook his head. "None," he said positively.

"Just not here," Walton said. "Maybe soon." He nodded down at the stack of newspapers. "One day now our butcher boy will come home." He nodded surely. "He's restless. He moves around, city to city. I think he could be someone I sentenced, Dee. Or someone I committed to a mental institution. Someone who had reason to hate me. When he saw what was happening after Gracey was picked up he gave himself a small vacation, maybe to help me lose my job." He sighed. "But there were so many cases down the years. I tried checking them out, going through old files, but there were just too damned many."

Richey shook his head. "You'll put out your eyes reading old files and all those newspapers. There's a lot of misery in the world, a lot of bad, bad people. You sentenced thousands of people, granted judgments against thousands more. You should have given Gracey the death penalty. I couldn't believe it when you didn't. The meanest, toughest judge in the city gives thirty years instead of the death penalty?" He shook his head. "The death penalty would have satisfied the voting mob."

"So I could be judge again? So I could sit on the bench and watch the world go more wrong every day?"

"It's the only world we own and your law is the only answer we have," Richey said defensively.

"For you and for me maybe. But not for those victims out there. How many murders are there a year? Better, how many get away with it? How many do we catch who thereafter get off in court or on appeal? So I was supposed to sentence a kid already half-dead from drugs to death to save myself politically?" Walton grinned sarcastically. "In the name of humanity?"

Richey nodded soothingly. "Yes. In the name of humanity. But you didn't so let's forget it all and go out on the town—on me. I'll buy you drinks and a steak. I can see I'm not going to get any drinks here. Maybe a bit of good free bourbon and some red meat will bring you to your senses and tomorrow you'll find one of those firms that offered you a soft job and take it."

Walton smiled. "Booze has never made me sensible yet, but I herewith accept your offer and we have a contract."

"Nothing has ever made you sensible," Richey said darkly. "You are the most single-minded, stubborn man I've ever met." He smiled, changing his whole face. "I can't understand why we get on well."

There were many crimes in other cities which captured Walton's eyes. He carefully clipped each one from the paper and looked daily for follow-up stories. He kept a folder of possibles and probables. When someone was caught and charged with a crime he'd clipped he excised that one from the files.

In Louisville an unknown blade wielder cut the throat and sliced off the nose of an old woman who lived alone. In Indianapolis, a hundred miles north of Louisville, a male in a ski mask attacked an aging night clerk in a fleabag hotel with a hatchet or meat cleaver, killing him, then cutting off his right hand. Mutilation was the key, the trademark for the man Walton's city had called "the Butcher." Usually a hand or arm, but sometimes, in the very old or female, some other, more bizarre part.

In Chicago, the following week, someone set fire to an old alcoholic as he lay sleeping in an alley. Walton listed that one as a maybe. There were a lot of maybes.

Walton's clippings crisscrossed the land, North, West, and South. But not East, not here. Now and then Walton gleaned something for his file from an Eastern newspaper, but nothing he could call a probable. The file grew bulky.

It was someone who had to kill, hated the old, existed to savage and mutilate them. Someone who'd lived at least part of his life in Walton's city and then had decided to roam until the death heat died down. And perhaps, Walton conjectured, someone who personally hated him. There were lots of people who hated him, a legion of them. He'd ruled his court with a heavy hand, scornful of plea bargains, available for trial, raging against a permissive system, handing out tough sentences, screaming at parole authorities. Twice he'd petitioned the legislature for more and tougher prisons without result.

Walton sat in his big chair and remembered the Gracey trial. There'd been demonstrations outside the courthouse, death threats on Gracey. Citizen committees had met. Before

Gracey was charged there'd been block watches, stepped-up police patrols, cops in drag and disguise walking the dark streets. When Leonard Gracey had been caught with his hands in a mutilated victim's pocket and a bloody ax nearby the city had rejoiced and collectively hated Gracey. Three people had been caught trying to enter Walton's courtroom with guns.

And then Walton, after a short, vindictive trial, had given Gracey only a thirty-year sentence and publicly stated he'd have liked it if he'd not had to pass even that sentence.

They'd mashed Walton the following November. The voters had chewed him up and spit him out, used up, discarded. It still enraged him to remember it. He knew he was right. And even though the system was frail and fallible he missed his part in it.

It got unseasonably warm in late March and Walton took to wandering the streets. He carried a heavy cane and learned to be adept with it. In a leg holster he wore a .32 Derringer with the bone handles removed for slimness. Richey arranged for the permit for that.

"If you're going to wander the streets down there you'd better go armed," he said and shook his head as if Walton were demented.

Walton found some special places. There were derelict bars by the river, bars where you could buy cheap liquor for forty cents a shot, wine for a quarter. There were drug dealers and men who dealt in young women and pretty boys. There were flophouses where you could stay overnight for a dollar. There were apartments like Walton's, places for forgotten men and women or those seeking forgetfulness.

Walton had the clippings of all the old Canning killings, times and dates and places. He concentrated his efforts in the general locality where killings had happened before. He became a part of the background of the area, a frail old man who apparently needed his cane to walk, who abused alcohol. And drink he did, carefully at first, less carefully later, yielding to a lifelong desire he'd been able to control as a judge. But every morning, hangover or not, he awoke to do an hour of calisthenics, working until he was sweating well, until his heart pounded against his ribs. Keeping fit, keeping ready.

Twice he was set upon. The first time it was a lone strong-arm robber who shadowed him back to his apartment and then tried to break in only to find Walton waiting, Derringer in hand. Walton was disappointed when the man had no weapon on him—a common robber preying through strength on the elderly.

The second time it was a gang of kids. They had him down and had taken his cane and were rolling him before he realized what they were about. A shot from the .32 dispersed them, but not before Walton took a nasty blow to the head which left him dizzy for days.

Dee Richey visited him again after that one.

"You're going to get yourself killed," he said, shaking his head.

Walton shook his head wryly. "Here I got you a strong-arm robber in the act, one who'd been giving you fits, here I break up one of your Canning kid gangs, put the fear of the Almighty in them, and you think I'll get killed."

Richey held out the case report and tapped it. "I read about the kids here, John. You're fortunate they didn't bash your head all the way in. You're lucky they were twelve- and thirteen-year-olds. There are older gangs in the area. Merciless gangs."

"I'll be all right."

Richey gave him a wise look. "No you won't. My officers report they see you staggering out of wino bars carrying a load which is far too heavy for you. You put the Butcher in prison, believe that. It's a fact. He's there. But someone else out there can and will kill you. Give it up, John. Go back to work you know or retire for good."

"I'm waiting, Dee. I need to do what I'm doing."

"Waiting for what?"

Walton shook his head. "He's coming back, Dee. The Butcher's coming back. It's spring out there. There are birds building nests, the trees are beginning to leaf out. I can almost feel him moving back this way. I know him. He cost me my job and I liked my job for all its problems, so I found out more than anyone else has ever known about him. He's coming back—soon."

"I should sign commitment papers on you," Richey said in disgust.

Five days later Walton was certain he was right.

The first killing was a bag lady who slept, in good weather, on a bench in a small park which overlooked the river. Other people also slept in the same park on other benches, but the old woman, Magda Lupoff, had owned the river-view bench for two years by right of conquest. She was mean and old and crazy and she carried a set of grass shears in her purse. Walton had seen her and knew vaguely who she was.

The Butcher hacked her throat through before she could cry out or get to her grass shears. When she was dead he sliced off both of her ears and planted one in each of her precious bags of possessions.

Walton called Dee Richey. "He's back."

"We think it's maybe a copycat," Richey demurred. "It was a hot night. Other people coveted that bench. We're questioning a lot of people, mostly bums."

"The people out there on the streets say it's him—that he's returned."

"The people out there aren't capable of making rational judgments."

Walton snorted. "Wake up, Dee. Get your people out on the streets. Maybe this time you'll catch him before he kills half a dozen."

The afternoon papers reported the story on an inner page and made no comment about the mutilation.

Walton went out early that night. All night long he wandered the streets, humming a little song as he crept along, using his cane to feel his way through the night. He drank nothing.

The night was uneventful. Walton continued the routine. At the bars he visited he'd buy a glass of wine and hover over it for half an hour, warming it with his hands, spilling it little by little, watching the crowd around him for new faces. There were some. People came and went. People died or moved on. New faces replaced old.

On a morning two days later, when Walton returned to his apartment, he found Dee Richey waiting for him. A police car was in front of the building with a uniformed driver at the wheel.

"Get in," Richey ordered from the rear window.

Walton got in. The uniformed driver put the car in gear and drove.

"We got another dead one. I want to show him to you," Richey said.

They drove to a place Walton recognized, near the bars, near the river. There were patrol cars with flashing red lights. There was a morgue wagon.

The old man lay in an alley. A bottle of cheap wine was

near his right hand. His right hand was near his body, but separated from it. He'd been hacked about the head.

"You know him?" Richey asked.

"Hard to tell. I don't recognize him."

"One of our people who was watching said he was standing next to you in a bar by the river last night, that you talked to him."

"I talk to anyone. I talk and I watch. Why are your people watching me?"

"We're not. But we have people out in that area."

"I see," Walton said, not sure whether he was being watched or not.

Richey shook his head and looked down at the body. "He's been dead since about midnight. I thought maybe you might have seen someone follow him out of the bar."

"No." Walton leaned toward the body and shook his head. "Why him and not me?" he asked.

Richey shook his head and asked his own questions. "Why does he cut off men's hands? With women he's playful. He does roguish little amputations like noses and ears. But with men it's hands. Sometimes he leaves the weapon, sometimes he takes it with him. Why?"

"He left one where you caught the Gracey kid," Walton said dryly.

The next day, for the first time in months, Walton bought no newspapers. There was no need.

At the first bar the next night Walton got himself a prop. He bought a bottle of cheap muscatel and carried it out into the streets with him. He carried it down alleys, spilling a bit here, a bit there, singing a little, staggering some.

Sometime that night he sensed a follower. There was someone behind, someone who lurked in shadows, a bulky person, but careful as an old fox. Once Walton caught a bit of an outline against dim light. The outline was vaguely wrong, too large on the left, too small on the right. That seemed to mean something to Walton, an old story, lost, and try as he would he couldn't remember what it was.

Walton waited down lonely alleys, but no one came. There was only someone out there shadowing him cautiously. He wondered if it might be a cop that Richey had put on him and hoped it wasn't.

At dawn Walton returned home. All day long he stayed awake in high excitement, hoping the follower would try to enter the apartment. But no one came.

At dusk he went back to the same bar, stayed there for a time, and then bought himself a new bottle and staggered out with it. He went down a dark, deserted alley and sat against a wall and went through drinking motions, letting the warm wine trickle into his mouth, then coughing and spitting it out.

There was nothing and then he sensed that there was something. Someone in the shadows.

The man appeared in front of him, looking down at him. Walton looked up, keeping his eyes half closed.

"My bottle," he said to the man defensively. He saw why the figure had seemed wrong. The right arm was gone near the shoulder, but the left seemed strong. The man carried his left hand under a windbreaker. His movements were quick and purposeful.

The man smiled. "I thought I recognized you. Today I went to the courthouse and asked about you. They said you'd moved down here after you got beat. You're Judge Walton. Do you remember me?"

The face was vaguely familiar, but Walton shook his head blearily. He held the wine away from the man as if afraid it would be taken. "My bottle," he said again.

"You committed me years ago," the man said. "My name's George Taine."

Walton searched his memory.

Taine extended his right stump a bit. "They did this to me one night there in the asylum, Judge. I was asleep and a crazy old man you'd also sent there got hold of a fire ax. He took my arm off." He stopped and studied Walton. "Do you remember now? Believe me, I remember you."

Walton nodded. He did remember, but not the way Taine had told it. The way he recalled it Taine had attempted to go over a wall at the mental hospital where they kept the criminally insane and had lost his arm to a shotgun blast when he'd tried to knife a guard who got in the way. After that, Walton remembered, Taine had escaped from the hospital where he'd been sent to recover from the wound. Years ago now and never found, never captured.

Taine's good hand came out of the jacket. The weapon this time was a meat cleaver. It glistened in the dark. Walton raised his cane defensively and Taine took a foot off the end of it contemptuously, the cleaver singing through the night air, its bite as sharp as the keenest knife, the arm aiming it swift and deadly sure.

Walton threw the rest of the cane at Taine. Instinctively the younger man dodged. By that time Walton had the pistol. He fired it hurriedly one time as Taine lunged at him. Taine slipped to the pavement.

Walton went to the man. The .32 slug had only grazed Taine's head and he was breathing. Walton pushed the cleaver away. He raised the Derringer and pointed it at Taine's head. One more shot. He saw that the man's eyes were open.

"Can you do it, Judge?" Taine asked him. "I can do it, but can you?"

Walton felt sweat break out and run down his back. He tried hard to squeeze the trigger.

"Remember. I'll be back," Taine whispered, smiling.

From far away Walton could hear a distant siren. He looked down at Taine. The man would be back. Walton remembered he'd committed him because Taine had killed before, some kind of family thing, his aged father. There'd be hearings. The legal system had a hundred thousand loopholes for crazies. Taine would be recommitted. The state asylums weren't very secure, weren't made for people like Taine. No place was.

Walton found he could not pull the trigger.

There was another way to end it.

Walton waited until the sound of the siren drew near. Then he picked up the cleaver and raised it high, its razor's edge aimed not at Taine's head, but lower, between the elbow and shoulder of the sole remaining arm.

Fifty Chinese

My law partner, the Senator, said in a reasonable voice, "You can't get a change of prosecutor, Robak."

I nodded, knowing that. Under our state's rules of procedure, where you allege bias, you can get a change of judge in a criminal case, but the judge wasn't our problem. The prosecutor, Timothy Toy, was.

"I know it's not the law, Senator." I frowned and gave him back one of his own favorite sayings which he sometimes used when things weren't legally going his way. "But it ought to be. There's truly a great need for it."

We were sitting in the Senator's office and discussing the upcoming murder trial of Richmond Clement.

"First time I ever heard of a defendant passing a lie detector test and the prosecution not giving it any credence at all," the Senator mused, somewhat scandalized. "It sort of shakes your faith in the system."

I brooded about that for a time on his old leather couch while he went back to reading something in *Corpus Juris Secundum*. In many ways he was a disorganized man. Books were piled in corners, stacked high on his desk, shelved in a disorderly fashion, and even in half a dozen messes on his floor. It wasn't that he was a careless man. Like someone who has taught the first grade for fifty years, he knew. It was only that he never seemed to complete a job of research.

Outside it was the cold of mid-winter. The jail had been chilly when I'd visited there half an hour before.

I'd also earlier argued a motion in *limine* in Judge

Steinmetz's court, a motion filed by the state. The motion was to keep me from mentioning, in any fashion, the results of any lie detector tests, asking any questions about any lie detector tests on *voir dire,* or of any witness, or calling any polygraph expert.

Within me was the sinking feeling that the good judge, who knew the law, would grant the state's motion in due time.

The Senator looked up from his book and became aware I was still there. "Tell me again what they've got in the way of evidence?" He leaned back in his old chair and grinned at me through yellowed dentures.

"No direct evidence except the one eyeball witness. Richmond Clement and the deceased were two of a kind, both of them cantankerous and mean. They owned adjoining farms and there had been several boundary disputes, some fence repair arguments, and general acrimony ever since they became neighbors ten years ago. The deceased was Howard Ryan and he was married, prior to his demise, to the good prosecutor's great aunt, Lara Toy Ryan. Mrs. Ryan says she watched Richmond Clement come onto the Ryan property, saw him argue with her husband, and then saw him shotgun Ryan down with a twelve gauge belonging to Ryan which he conveniently kept in his barn." I nodded, remembering. "There are some very ugly pictures."

"Fingerprints?"

"None. Richmond was arrested and immediately claimed he'd not done it. I arranged a lie detector, and he passed it." I smiled. "Thereafter we offered to let the state police test him with both sides being bound by the results and Toy declined. Says he doesn't believe in polygraphs any more."

"Could the wife have done it?"

"Anyone could have. Ryan wasn't a gentle man. Any

passer by, any wandering stranger, any old enemy could have done it. Richmond claims, and I feel, that he's just the most likely suspect, so Mrs. Ryan picked him. He has no alibi. And she hates him, mostly because her husband hated him I'd guess. She's an old lady. I took her deposition and got lots of sighs and tears and venom."

"Smoke screen?" he asked.

"Perhaps. I don't know."

"I've known the Toy family around this town and county for all my life. They usually live to be ninety or a hundred years old. As a family they share certain traits, they're all mean and they're all vengeful. I'm sure you've had enough problems with the prosecutor to agree with that?"

I nodded. He could be right, but Lara Toy Ryan had moved like a careful old dog out for a stroll the day I'd deposed her. And all I'd gotten deposing her was of no value.

"What else?" he asked.

"There are maybe a dozen witnesses to the Clement-Ryan arguments and threats. Our man drinks a bit. He'd threatened to shoot Ryan in a lot of area bars." I nodded. "I told Toy I'd plead Richmond guilty to having a bad temper."

"How about her eyesight?"

"That's one bright thing. It's only fair. She wears glasses and had a cataract removed from her right eye a year ago. Her eye doctor slipped me the word that she sees pretty well with her glasses when she wears them. He didn't know if she wore them all the time." I thought for a moment. "My bet is she'll swear she had them on whether she did or not. I wondered a little, during her deposition, whether she ever really saw anything at all?"

"Hmmmmmmph," Senator Adams said, clearing his throat and looking out his fogged window. Now it was snowing. He took off his own glasses and polished them with a frayed handkerchief. He wasn't a very neat man. "When did this murder supposedly happen?"

"Last October. No tracks in or out, a dry cool day." I shook my head, frustrated. "So my man says he didn't do it, takes a polygraph and passes it, and is still on the hook because he's all the prosecutor's got. Besides, Toy's dear uncle is dead and his aunt teary eyed and vindictive."

"Did Clement do it?"

"He says not."

"Has he paid us?"

"Adequately if not munificently. He put a mortgage on his farm to come up with the money." I struck my palm with the fist of my other hand. "What we have is one mean, nasty old defendant as our only witness."

"Married?"

"Divorced. A long time ago."

"Has the prosecutor made you any offer?"

"Thirty years. At Richmond's age that would be life for him."

"Well, it does sort of shake your faith in the system," he said again. "Let me think on it overnight and we'll talk some more tomorrow." He looked up at me keenly. "Are the sheriff and the prosecutor still on the outs?"

I nodded. "Yes, sir. That's my only source of encouragement. The sheriff looked over the jury list with me. And he kind of likes Richmond for some reason I can't fathom."

"The story I hear is that Prosecutor Toy is backing the sheriff's chief deputy for the office in the upcoming spring primary."

"Yes. That's why they fell out."

He tapped a gnarled, old finger against his desktop. "Did you ever hear me tell the story about the fifty Chinese?"

He had a thousand stories. Some of them I'd heard many

times, but I didn't remember a Chinese story. I shook my head resignedly.

"I'll tell you about it later," he said, perhaps reading my mood. "Richmond Clement has some brothers around here, doesn't he?"

"Yes, sir. Two of them. One's six years older and lives here in town. The other is four years younger and lives next county north."

"Have you seen them?"

I nodded.

"Would they resemble Richmond?"

"There's a strong family resemblance. The older brother would outweigh Richmond thirty pounds, the younger one is Richmond's build, but maybe three or four inches shorter."

"Chinese," the Senator said softly. He looked down at a turnip watch. "It's time for me to retire to the downtown Moose for Bourbon and branch. Join me? We'll think some more on this."

"Not tonight," I said. "I guess I'll look over instructions and try to dig out some more good law on motions in *limine*."

"You'd do as much good drinking Bourbon and branch," he said, grinning again through his dentures.

I shook my head.

"One more thing then. Did you check to see if Mr. and Mrs. Ryan were getting along in their marriage?"

I nodded. "I couldn't find anything to indicate otherwise. Still I'll whack her with that on the stand if I think there's any chance to create confusion. She came over very meek and surprised and tearful and mad on the deposition."

He nodded. "Cunning. Toys are mean and cunning." He shook his head. He didn't like Prosecutor Toy any better than I did.

★ ★ ★ ★ ★

In the morning I had an early surprise. Richmond Clement's two brothers awaited me at the office.

"Senator Adams called last night and asked us to come in early," the younger one, Arthur Clement, said. The older one, William, nodded stolidly.

Virginia, our peerless secretary, shook her head. "He's not in yet." She gave me a nasty look. "And if you don't stop getting him into criminal cases at his age, the day'll soon come when he doesn't make it in at all."

I nodded contritely. If there was a pecking order in the office, it started at Virginia, then moved on to the Senator, then lastly to me.

"I didn't even know he'd asked these men to come in," I mumbled. I was saved from further secretarial harangue by the arrival of the Senator. He was freshly barbered for a change and he had a man with him whose face was vaguely familiar.

"You men come into my office," he said.

Virginia frowned at her exclusion and went back to her typewriter, pounding it savagely.

"This is Lester Shay," the Senator said, introducing his companion. "And these are the brothers of the man I just showed you in the jail. This, of course, is my young associate, Don Robak."

"You run a local beauty parlor," I said brightly, remembering his name and face from somewhere.

"Lester does a bit more than that," the Senator said. "He's a cosmetologist and a barber and more. He worked for a while in New York at one of the theaters there doing make-up and the like. He's the make-up man for the River Players group locally. He's as close as we'll get in Bington to what we need."

Lester smiled conspiratorially, still sizing up the two

Clement brothers. "Close enough, I hope."

"Can you do anything with these two?"

"I can try. There are possibilities."

"You're going to try to make them up to look like Richmond?" I asked.

"Not exactly," the Senator said. "I do have an immediate task for you. I'd like you to seek private conference with Judge Steinmetz. Tell him I'm into this with you. Try to get him to trade your loss of the motion in *limine* for the right to have these two brothers kept and brought from the jail during the trial each day with Richmond. You can tell him the sheriff has approved it. If I know Steinmetz, he'll be upset at Toy keeping your polygraph testimony from the jury. So we'll give the prosecuting witness a line-up she can truly pick from."

I inspected the idea for flaws. "The chief deputy will surely know which one Richmond is. He'll tell Toy and Toy will tell her."

"Of course that will happen," he said. "The prosecutor is a devious man. We'll do some sleight of hand, Donald. The sheriff knows about that, too. He's enthusiastic about it."

I nodded. "I've got it. The sheriff will send the chief deputy somewhere else on business or maybe vacation?"

The Senator shook his head. "Wrong." He smiled. "Let me do it my way."

"You're going to take over the trial?" I asked.

"Let's say, instead, that I'm going to sit beside you while the trial is happening."

We began trial the following Monday morning. If Prosecutor Toy was dismayed when the sheriff brought over three defendants instead of one (Judge Steinmetz having agreeably consented), he gave no sign. He nodded at the chief deputy, who nodded back and, I thought, winked, and then began to wrangle with me about the jury selection.

We had a jury by noon.

I tried then to do my usual job. I was persnickety and contentious. I acted like a pup at a bird hunt. I objected to exhibits and questioned relevance and materiality. I doubted chain of custody. The Senator sat next to me, smiling and nodding. After all, he'd taught me. On the other side of the Senator sat the three brothers, also smiling and nodding, as if on cue from the Senator.

The rules of evidence are complicated, but Prosecutor Toy had done his homework well and he won most of the important arguments. I did manage to harry him into anger a number of times so that his perpetual courtroom scowl grew steadily deeper.

I knew, of course, which of the three my client was. If he'd been tampered with in any fashion by the Senator's make-up man/beauty operator, I could see no evidence of it. He had been instructed to smile instead of frown, but I'd done that early.

The younger brother, Arthur, had been extensively made up. His hair had been cut short, his eyebrows plucked down thin, and the Senator must have instructed him to frown instead of smile. It also seemed to me, when they brought him and removed him with the other two, that he was taller.

Prosecutor Toy showed the jury his inflammatory photos of a man shot in the head at close range by a shotgun. Steinmetz kept out the color photos, but let in black and whites. Toy paraded the death shotgun in front of the jury time after time, passed clear plastic envelopes containing buckshot extracted from Ryan, let them dwell for almost a day on the testimony of a doctor who described in fearsome detail what had caused Ryan's death. Then he had them listen to ten different witnesses testify to overhearing

Richmond Clement threatening Ryan at various times.

It became obvious, after a time, that Prosecutor Toy was saving Mrs. Ryan as his final witness, to tie it all together by identifying Richmond Clement as the man who'd done the killing.

"Watch the time," the Senator said anxiously to me. "When Toy's done with her I want to be able, under the right circumstances, to forego most cross examination and go right to our case."

"How do you mean?" I whispered back, puzzled.

"I don't want them to finish with her in the late afternoon so we then have to wait until next day. I want her to make her identification and then us go on right then." He smiled at me. "You know which one Richmond is, don't you?"

"Sure. You didn't change him any."

He smiled mysteriously and I was momentarily unsure. I looked down the row of three and was sure again.

The Senator was getting up in years. I sighed to myself. Maybe a touch of senility.

They put Lara Toy Ryan on the stand as the first witness on the sixth day of the trial. She had a high-pitched voice which I remembered, but she seemed stronger than when I'd deposed her. I wondered again, as I had before: Could she have killed her husband?

It became obvious early she was out for Richmond's blood.

"I saw it all. My husband never had a chance," she wailed.

I objected and had it stricken and the jury admonished, but I knew that what she'd said, like the ghastly photos, had made an impression on the jury. They seemed to me as if they were only waiting for their time to come so they could dash to the jury room and convict Richmond Clement.

Toy said, "And now, Mrs. Ryan, we have reached a point in the trial that all of us have been waiting for anxiously. Please look over at the defense table."

She did.

"Notice that defense counsel have three men seated beside them in an obvious effort to cause you identification problems. Is there a problem?"

"No, sir."

"Do you know which of those three men shot and killed your husband?"

"Of course I do."

"Do you see all right, Mrs. Ryan?"

"With glasses my vision is close to normal. And I was right up there at the window watching from behind the curtain when it happened, only twenty feet or so away from the barn door."

"And you had a plain view of the killer?"

"Yes."

"Will you point out the killer?"

"I certainly will." She gazed down our row of three Clement brothers and without any hesitation picked out Richmond's younger brother as the killer.

Prosecutor Toy smirked at us. "No more questions."

The Senator nudged me and whispered, "Ask her if she's completely positive of her identification. Act like you're downcast and upset about it." He tapped me on the knee. "Quick now."

I did as he directed. I sat there shaking my head for a moment and then looked down at the table. "No more questions."

"The State rests," Toy said.

I let the Senator call our one witness to the stand. While he examined him I watched Mrs. Ryan.

"Your name?" the Senator asked.

"Arthur Clement."

"Where do you live and what do you do?"

"I live in Missouri County, one north of here, and I'm mostly a farmer, but sometimes I preach a little."

"Are you a married man?"

"I sure hope so, sir. I've got ten children."

Several jurors laughed. Mrs. Ryan jumped when they did. She whispered something to Toy.

"You're not the defendant in this case?" the Senator asked.

"Not me, sir. My brother over there, Richmond, he's the defendant. He lives next to where Mr. Ryan used to live."

"Point out Richmond for the jury." Arthur did and the Senator had Richmond stand.

"Does he look any different now than he did on the day he was supposed to have killed Mr. Ryan?"

"He ain't changed," Arthur said, grinning a little.

Prosecutor Toy was raging. "We know they changed him over in the jail, Judge Steinmetz. That one on the stand is lying. I know . . ."

Steinmetz shook his head, stopping Toy. "I've known Richmond Clement for close to forty years and this witness isn't Richmond Clement." He smiled gently at the now enraged Toy. "You want to dismiss this or do you want me to direct a verdict, Mr. Toy?"

We sat in the office the next day. The celebration had gone on too long the night before. Even the sheriff had joined us for one drink, which soon became five or six, at the downtown Moose.

"Tell me once more, slowly, how you did it?" I asked.

"Well I got to thinking about the story of the fifty Chinese," the senator said. "A lawyer in San Francisco was defending a Chinaman accused of theft. On the day of the trial he brought fifty Chinese men into the courtroom and had them sit with him and his client. No one could identify the defendant, and so he got off. It's an old story."

"I'd never heard it," I admitted. "But you didn't change Richmond Clement at all."

"There I played on the suspicions of Prosecutor Toy. We made the chief deputy think we did. We even let him watch some of the early work. He saw Lester Shay take Richmond and his brothers into a room. In the room Lester performed some work on Richmond. He lightly trimmed his hair and used pins to put it up so it looked much shorter. Then, later, after the chief deputy had been sent on, Shay did severely cut Arthur's hair. Shay used bleach on Clement's eyebrows and then darkened them again when the chief deputy was gone. He thinned Arthur's eyebrows and used bleach on them. He put Arthur into elevator shoes. Most important, we made Clement smile all the time after that night and made Arthur frown. The chief deputy took what he knew to the prosecutor. I bragged to him that we were going to make Arthur look so much like Richmond no one would ever know. That was enough. Toys are devious people, Don, so the plot had to be devious. We made Arthur look like what they thought Richmond would be." He looked moodily out his window, not completely happy about the deception. "I'd not have helped if Toy had let the lie detector in." He shook his head. "It won't work again in my lifetime, and it wouldn't have worked this time if the sheriff and the prosecutor hadn't been angry with each other."

"It saved Richmond's goose."

"On Ryan's wife, I understand she took it all very badly," the Senator said slyly.

"I watched her while you were questioning Arthur. She wasn't happy."

"It got worse. The bailiff told me she smacked her nephew with her purse in the hall and said he was the one who'd told her which one Richmond was. Cussed him good and mean. All this didn't make the prosecutor any happier and may even have made him angry. I understand he's now wanting her to take a lie detector test, relative or not."

"How do you know that?"

"She called here for you, but got me. She'd like us to represent her in any further difficulties. She sounded a little worried."

"What did you tell her?"

"I told her we'd represent her." He smiled. "And I advised her she need not take any lie detector test. After all, from what the prosecutor himself has pronounced, they aren't reliable evidence in this county."